Jessica fixed Jež with a sharp eye.

To his credit, the man did not squirm.

"Jež," Jessica said, loud enough to be heard several rows back. "In one word, what is the status of *Auberon* for combat operations?"

The man blinked once, a poker player suddenly keeping his cards close to the vest. "Ready."

"Good enough for now, Centurion Jež," she replied.

"Ma'am?" he said, confused enough to break character for the first time. The other officers also began to look less solemn, like perhaps this wasn't going to be an execution, after all.

Or maybe it was.

"The correct answer is *hungry*," she announced loudly. "This is a warship of the *Republic of Aquitaine*, ladies and gentlemen. We are about to go to war."

Auberon
The Jessica Keller Chronicles: Volume One
Blaze Ward
Copyright © 2015 Blaze Ward
All rights reserved
Published by Knotted Road Press
www.KnottedRoadPress.com

ISBN: 978-0692413401

Cover art:
© Innovari | Dreamstime.com - Escort Spaceships Photo

Cover and interior design copyright © 2015 Knotted Road Press

Never miss a release!
If you'd like to be notified of new releases, sign up for my newsletter.

I only send out newsletters once a quarter, will never spam you, or use your email for nefarious purposes. You can also unsubscribe at any time.

http://www.blazeward.com/newsletter/

AUBERON

THE JESSICA KELLER CHRONICLES:
VOLUME ONE

BLAZE WARD

Knotted Road Press
www.KnottedRoadPress.com

ALSO BY BLAZE WARD

Collections

Beyond the Mirror: Volume 1 Fantastic Worlds
Beyond the Mirror: Volume 2 Fantastic Worlds
Beyond the Mirror: Volume 3 Alternate Worlds

Science Fiction Stories

The Earthquake Gun
Greater Than The Gods Intended
The Librarian
Moscow Gold
Myrmidons

Javier Aritza Stories

The Science Officer
The Mind Field

Brak Stories

Destiny
The Meat Shield
The Popcorn Kitten

Kaleph Stories

The Changestorm
Death Key for the Great Khan

Suren Stories

The Horse Thief
The Slave Market

Zolnerovy Stories

Valeryia
Tatiyana

AUBERON

THE JESSICA KELLER CHRONICLES:
VOLUME ONE

BLAZE WARD

Auberon Cast List

Auberon

Name	Rank	Position
Jessica Marie Keller	Command Centurion	Commander
Marcelle Augustine Travere	Yeoman	Jessica's Personal Aide
Denis August Jež	Senior Centurion	First Officer
Enej Zivkovic	Centurion	Flag Centurion
Tamara Strnad	Senior Centurion	Tactical Officer
Tobias Brewster	Centurion	Gunner/Emergency Tactical
Aleksander Afolayan	Centurion	Gunner
Nina Vanek	Centurion	Defenses
Nada Zupan	Centurion	Pilot
Vilis Ozolinsh	Senior Centurion	Chief Engineer
(Phillip) Navin Crncevic	Senior Centurion	Dragoon
Dr. Zephan Samara	Senior Centurion	Surgeon
Daniel Giroux	Centurion	Science Officer
Moirrey Kermode	Yeoman	Evil Engineering Gnome
Nicolai Aoiki	Senior Chef	Chief Chef of the Wardroom
Naoki Ungaretti	Yeoman	Diplomatic Courier
Augstine Kwok	Command Centurion	Former commander, *Auberon*

Others

Name	Rank	Position
Alber' d'Maine	Command Centurion	Commander, *Rajput*
Tomas Kigali	Command Centurion	Commander, *CR-264*

Pilots

Name	Rank	Position
Iskra Vlahovic	Senior Centurion	Flight Deck Commander
Jouster / Milos Pavlovich	Senior Flight Centurion	Flight Commander
Uller / Friedhelm Hannes Förstner	Flight Centurion	*Jouster's* Wingmate
Vienna / Avril Bouchard	Flight Centurion	*Jouster's* Wingmate
Southbound / Marta Eka	Senior Flight Centurion	Wing Commander
Ironside / Gustav Papp	Flight Centurion	*Southbound's* Wingmate
Bitter Kitten / Darya Lagunov	Flight Centurion	*Southbound's* Wingmate
da Vinci / Ainsley Barret	Senior Flight Centurion	Scout Pilot
Gaucho / Hollis Dyson	Flight Centurion	Commander, *Cayenne*
Anastazja Slusarczyk	Senior Flight Centurion	Commander, *Necromancer*

Republic Officials

Name	Position
Nils Kasum	First Lord of the Fleet
Kamil Miloslav	Personal Aide to First Lord Kasum
Bogdan Loncar	First Fleet Lord
Bogusław Tesar	Fleet Lord, retired
Tadej Marko Horvat	Premier, Republic Senate
Andjela Tomčič	Senator, Republic Senate
Brant	Aide to the Chairman
Milon Postovich	Sergeant At Arms, Republic Senate
Johnathon	Doorman, Loncar's Club
Matthias	Concierge, Loncar's Club
Samantha	Waitress, Loncar's Club

Imperial Officials

Name	Position
Dr. Yuda Alyona	Provost, *St. Albertus Magnus,* Independent Cantons of Wilankadu
His Sovereign Imperial Majesty Karl VII of the House of Wiegand	Emperor, *Fribourg Empire*
Prince Klaus Wiegand, Grand Duke	Younger Brother of Karl
Emmerich Wachturm	Admiral of the Red. Hereditary Duke of Eklionstic. Commander, *Amsel*
Hans Huff	Grand Admiral, Chief of Naval Operations
Kunibert Marquering	Admiral of the Blue
Sigmund Dittmar	Captain, Imperial Naval Staff
Reinner Rapp	Captain, Imperial Naval Staff
Artur Marquering	Admiral of the White
Gunther Wachturm	Captain, Imperial Naval Staff
Hendrik Baumgärtner	Flag Captain, Aide to Admiral Wachturm
Henrietta (Heike) Wachturm	Daughter of Emmerich Wachturm
Tomas	Day Flight Control, 2218 Svati Prime
Evgeny	Swing Flight Control, 2218 Svati Prime

CHAPTER I

Imperial Founding: 170/09/04. St. Legier

Emmerich waited stoically outside the conference room door, the maroon of his Admiral Of The Red dress uniform contrasting nicely with the gold theme of the walls, standing at parade rest. It was hard not to fret. The two guards protecting the door were entirely professional, down to the light battle rifles each had hung from a sling.

He knew better than to read too much into their posture, nor their presence. That was normal, as those things went. His Sovereign Imperial Majesty, Karl VII, House Wiegand, Sovereign Lord of the *Fribourg Empire*, Grand Duke of *St. Legier*, Supreme Commandant of the Imperial Navy, and about a hundred other titles, equally long and equally interesting, at least to historians, sat on the other side of that door.

He would be invited inside soon enough.

No. Strike that. Now.

Emmerich watched the door open on silent glass hinges, carefully counter-weighted against its immense mass.

A man in a dark blue Captain's uniform stood at the door and fixed him with a stare. It wasn't hostile, predominantly. Cousin Reiner was just a serious person, engaged in serious business. This was a serious day.

"Admiral Wachturm," he called. The words had a formal cant to them, as was to be expected with the door to the chamber open. Appearances had to be kept up, at all costs. "His Majesty will see you now."

Reiner disappeared back a step into the room. Emmerich came out of his parade rest and stepped across the hall. Inside the chamber it was better than he hoped. And worse.

Seven men around a conference table. The big kind, cut and polished out of a single piece of blue granite, resting atop heavy wooden legs, dark with age and polish. The walls were rather plain, made from a dark jade covered with a few tapestries that represented particularly important battles in the founding and history of the Empire. It was a harsh room. These were harsh men.

His Imperial Majesty Karl VII. A tall, dour man with dark hair finally halfway gray and a beard that had long since passed. But for his own lack of a beard, Emmerich had been more than occasionally mistaken for the Emperor's younger brother Klaus.

At least today His Majesty was wearing the dark blue uniform of the Supreme Commandant, with the single spiral galaxy as a rank on each shoulder board, rather than the more formal Imperial robes of state. Hopefully, that meant something good.

Six other men around the table. Two uncles. Four cousins, not counting the Emperor. This gathering was the Imperial Fleet. There might be an Admiral's Counsel, down two stories and in a different wing of the palace, but they handled administrative tasks. Here, in this room, resided control of the *Fribourg Empire*. Or, at least, the Imperial Navy, and that was almost the same thing.

Grand Admiral Huff, Operational Chief of the Naval Staff, occasionally Uncle Hans, rose from his chair and rapped the table for attention.

"Sergeant At Arms," he called in a clear baritone, the kind intended to be heard across a burning deck in the middle of battle, "Clear and lock the room."

Two guards detached themselves from just inside the door. Two more joined them from the far end.

It was an impressive ritual. Every man in the room, including the Emperor himself, was inspected against his credentials badge, then against the records of the Imperial Marines, and personally authorized to remain behind. The four marines closed the door behind them as they left.

Emmerich listened to the quiet sound as blast bars locked the vault-like door into position. It sounded like doom whispered in the still air.

Several moments passed, Emmerich staring at his kin wordlessly. Them staring back.

"Em," Grand Admiral Huff began, pointing to an empty chair on one side. "Sit down and tell us what really happened at the Battle of Iger…"

CHAPTER II

It was a comfortable place, his home away from home for several years. Emmerich Wachturm, Admiral of the Red, stood at the flag console of his Battleship, *Imperial Fighting Vessel (IFV) Amsel.* Around him, a quiet, competent crew worked at their stations, lending the space a calm that eluded him.

He scowled at the politician on the communications screen through heavy, lidded eyes. He suppressed the exasperated sigh that threatened to escape his lips.

"As I have already told you, Governor," he felt stupid repeating himself, but the man apparently just was not willing to let an original thought enter his head. "There are not enough vessels available to station them as you demand. The orbital platforms will just have to defend themselves. I cannot imagine that the *Republic of Aquitaine* cares enough about you personally to threaten your investments. And I do not have enough ships to evacuate them. Goodbye and good luck."

He stabbed the button to sever the connection as if poking the idiot bureaucrat in the eye. That would have made him feel a little better. It would not have done much good, but there was not much about this day that he could do.

A hand, once across the face as if scraping away a layer of flesh. So much to do, if he was going to salvage this situation. How had they managed to be caught so far off guard?

Emmerich looked at the man across the console from him, quieting waiting for his turn to speak. He fixed his aide, his Flag Captain, with a tired stare. "What is the status of the enemy fleet?"

The man glanced down once, not long enough to read anything, but enough to confirm the numbers on the table before him. Always a professional.

"We have a probable on two Republic Fleet Carriers, one of them possibly *Ajax*, plus a regular fleet of escorts and consorts. According to Imperial Intelligence, the First Fleet Lord should be Loncar."

Emmerich nodded to himself. He muttered under his breath, but the men were used to his habits. "And just enough time to throw me into the breach and ask me to pull out a miracle," he growled under his breath. "What is the status of *Black Widow*?"

"The Republic escorts have been finding and smashing the probes we left behind," the captain said, "but as of an hour ago, they had sorted themselves out, arrayed to battle in their usual formations, and launched their assault waves. Those fighters should be reaching the outermost *Iger* system defenses in another eighteen minutes, sir. Nothing from *Black Widow* as of yet."

Emmerich felt his first smile of the day. Count on Fleet Lord Loncar to fall for it. A surprise thrust at a weakly-defended Imperial system by a major Republic fleet. Surprise across the board, only barely thwarted by routine Imperial Intelligence operations and the luck of his squadron being close enough to get here first.

The captain gave him a concerned look. He leaned in.

"What is it?" Emmerich asked, all serious now that battle was at hand.

"*Black Widow* is likely to be annihilated, Admiral," the man said quietly, so quietly that nobody else on the bridge could hear.

Emmerich leaned in as well. This wasn't a conversation to have in public, but Flag Captain Baumgärtner had been with him for several years. "*Black Widow* was going to be annihilated when they got out of bed this morning, Hendrik. It would have been 24 on 54, and them on the defensive. At least this way, they stand a very good change of destroying two Republic Fleet Carriers and smashing the entire enemy campaign in one afternoon."

CHAPTER III

Imperial Founding: 170/08/04. St. Legier

"So what happened at that point, Em?" Uncle Hans asked. He seemed curious rather than hostile. Perhaps the Emperor hadn't decided to retire Emmerich to Academy life, just yet.

"As clearly as we can tell," Emmerich replied, "the surprise was only partial. It is possible someone sent a signal that was deciphered at the last moment. As soon as the fighter squadrons that made up the *Black Widow* element came over the pole of the third moon, they encountered the Republic destroyer squadron moving across to intercept. That force had been on the lee-side of the fleet from the moon and the ambush, but managed to get into position fast enough save the carriers. The attacking Republic fighters were recalled but could not affect the outcome of that battle. Damage across the Republic fleet was still significant before *Black Widow* was destroyed. The *Republic of Aquitaine* fleet packed up and fled. *Iger* was saved."

The Emperor had been sipping coffee from a mug that had been a present from a niece as he listened. He leaned forward now, eyes intent and narrowed. His brow furrowed in concentration. "Could it have been a trap to destroy *Black Widow* and two squadrons of fighters?"

Emmerich shrugged. He had thought the same until he played back the logs. "Possibly, Sire," he said carefully. His Majesty was touchy about certain things. "I would find it an amazingly high price to pay, considering one Fleet Carrier significantly damaged, and three destroyers mauled. Had the destroyers been on the left flank instead of the right, they would have crushed *Black Widow* at very little risk to themselves. As it was, I have a very grainy image of what we think is the lead destroyer physically ramming one damaged fighter and getting its nose scorched, rather than letting the craft explode near the other carrier."

The Emperor leaned back and scanned the room. Emmerich held his breath. The eventual Court of Inquiry would be a mere formality. The next words would actually be his fate. All eyes watched His Majesty.

"I think," Karl began, "that We owe you yet another debt of gratitude for saving the Empire, Em."

"Sire," Emmerich nodded, face down to keep anyone from seeing his eyes light up. Hopefully he wouldn't be forced into retirement any time soon. There was nothing worse than a desk job.

"You and your crews were planning on a quiet sailing tour before all hell broke loose," Karl VII continued with a smile. "I think We can finally arrange that…"

CHAPTER IV

The closest image Jessica could think of to compare was a pod of whales, great gray beasts in all sizes arrayed below her as she watched.

She stood at the long plexisteel portal and looked down at the vastness of the immense orbital drydock and graving yard exposed below her. She snorted under her breath at the terms. There was neither water nor concrete involved, but the names had come into space with the sailors who manned them A careful, conservative lot.

That might be a problem shortly.

Her court-martial was almost concluded, but for the verdict. Her fate was in the hands of a group of Fleet Lords, who might or might not be on her side. This might be her last chance at this view.

For a moment, she considered the road that had gotten her here. The choices, the what-ifs, the things she barely whispered to herself in the dead of night, but had never shared with another soul. There was no other for her.

Or perhaps, she had simply never made the time, to look, to pause, the wonder. It was simply not in her makeup to rest, to relax, to engage in random frivolity.

It wasn't who she was. Even now.

Below, in the nearest bay, her own ship was berthed.

The *Republic of Aquitaine Navy* (*RAN*) Destroyer Leader *Brightoak* looked forlorn, with a massive number of panels opened down her flank. The entire bow section, at least what remained after the Battle of *Iger*, had been removed at the eighth frame, shortening the vessel by nearly a fifth.

The vessel would be here for a while, probably far longer than she.

Beyond it, in the humongous center bay, lay one of the greatest of the gray beasts, the Fleet Carrier *RAN Archon,* resting as if beached. Of the two Fleet Carriers, she had taken the most damage at *Iger*, and bore most of the scars. Not as many as *Brightoak*, but enough. The other Fleet Carrier *RAN Ajax* had gotten away almost unhurt, comparatively.

Jessica glanced at her faint reflection in the plexisteel. 1.6 meters tall. Green eyes. Brunette hair kept short for a suit. She'd tried blond for a while, but found it more effort that reward. Strong shoulders and thighs. Tendency to fleshiness if she didn't eat and exercise with mono-maniacal devotion.

Discipline.

The forest green dress uniform of the *Republic of Aquitaine* Navy was tight enough to show off her curves, with three white stripes for a Command Centurion encircling her right upper arm and *Brightoak's* patch on her left shoulder. For formal, official duties, she had all the tags on her right breast that indicated schools, certifications, and service. Because this wasn't for a cocktail party, none of the medals or awards she was entitled to wear were on the left.

Footsteps approached from behind, loud enough to draw her attention, not loud enough to be rude. She looked up at Marcelle's reflection as the woman got close.

Her steward, her *yeoman*, her aide. Yeoman Marcelle Travere was tall, over 1.85 meters, and elegant looking with short black hair. Or would have been if she had ever taken a notion to try. The Navy had become her life young and she had dedicated herself to it with single-minded devotion for better than two decades now.

Something else they shared.

Jessica wondered if Marcelle's career hung on the same threads hers did. Only one of them was being court-martialed today, but they might both go down with the same gavel.

"First Lord sent me to find you," the older woman said quietly with a wry smile. "He expects that it's about time. Figured I'd find you here, looking out on the ladies."

Jessica smiled at the implied joke. Neither of the women had really ever found the time to have men in their lives. Marcelle had never really cared one way or the other, or perhaps never really drawn any distinctions worth mentioning. Jessica had always been too busy. Too many things to do, places to go, things to see. Never time to slow down.

That might be about to change.

Jessica shrugged, glanced once more down at her ship, at least hers for a little while yet, and nodded. Yeoman Travere preceded her back down the long hallway without a glance back.

CHAPTER V

As the Bailiff of the Court rap his ceremonial staff on the floor once to get everyone's attention, silence rippled out like waves on a still pond.

Jessica was impressed. The courtroom was as packed with people as the Gendarme would allow. People filled every seat behind the railing that separated her from them.

In front of her, a single long table and five empty chairs.

"All rise," the Bailiff bounced the words off the back of the small auditorium. "This Court will return to session."

Like everyone else in the room, Jessica stood to watch the five Justices file slowly into the room, their decades of naval service lending even greater dignity and gravity to the scene. One by one, they stopped behind their seats and waited until the Bailiff rapped his staff again and they sat.

The room noisily did the same, and then quickly subsided.

The silence in the room was oppressive. Jessica had to fight the urge to look over her shoulder and see if everyone else was holding their breath as well. It would have looked bad, and her solicitor would have tapped her hand to bring her eyes back to the front anyway.

The Fleet Lord on the far right, the President of this Court, looked quietly out over the entire audience, dragging the silence to uncomfortable lengths. Pins would have been embarrassed to drop.

Finally, he looked down at the paper in front of him, as if seeing if for the first time.

"The defendant, Command Centurion Jessica Marie Keller, will rise," he commanded.

Jessica stood behind the table that had been her second home for the last three days. Her solicitor rose as well, and stepped back a step, leaving her alone to face them. Jessica was not offended. The man had done a splendid job presenting her case and protecting her command decisions from the prosecution.

But they both knew that this was going to be a political decision. And she just didn't know the five Justices on the court well enough to know how many of them were classified as *Fighting Lords*, and how many were *Noble Lords*. It was probably a fair mix.

How fair?

So she stood and came to parade rest, her hands crossed behind her, chin up, eyes challenging these men and women to do their worst. It was what she was best at.

"Centurion Keller," the president began in his grand, stentorian voice, "you have been accused of dereliction of duty and willfully disobeying a direct order by your lawful superior officer, in regards to what has been recorded as the Third Battle of *Iger*. You have pled not guilty."

He paused there to fix her with those great, beetling eyebrows, like an owl about to pounce on a field mouse.

The field mouse considered baring her teeth in response.

"This Court," he continued, "has heard all the necessary testimony, which is hereinafter entered into the record, and stands prepared to make final our judgment. Do you have anything further to say to this Court?"

Jessica took a quick, shallow breath through her nose and flexed the muscles quickly in her back, all the while standing as a marble statue.

"If it please the Court, your Honors," she said after a beat, nodding, "I do not."

The president nodded in satisfaction. He looked down at the paper before him once more before he looked up at her. She could see traces of triumph creeping into his eyes and his voice as he spoke.

Whose triumph?

"This Court finds the defendant…not guilty, and commands that the charges against her be struck from her record. Further…"

Whatever else he said was drowned by the sudden surge of cheers and noise behind her. Jessica would read the decision later. For now, she was mobbed by an impossibly large mass of well-wishers wanting to shake her hand, or touch her arm, or just say *thank you* to her.

Who were all these people?

She looked around for her solicitor, but the man had already been swallowed by the sea of humanity. Marcelle managed to elbow and jostle her way through the mess long enough to lean in close, just as a Fleet Lord Jessica had never met kissed her on both cheeks.

"*He* would like you to call upon him," Marcelle growled in her ear. Said that way, there was no real doubt as to who she meant. Jessica nodded, but knew it would be several minutes before she could escape the press.

What had she done to be so popular with so many people?

CHAPTER VI

Date of the Republic June 26, 392 Command Headquarters: Ladaux

It was a non-descript door, simply marked *2304*.

Jessica watched as Marcelle rapped firmly on the door with her knuckles and then stepped back and out of the way.

Marcelle gave her an automatic once-over before nodding. Jessica had not, after all, had time to muss her dress uniform, yet.

The day was young.

Jessica came to parade rest beside Marcelle and waited. The first half of her fate had already been decided, downstairs in that court room. The other half waited on the other side of this portal. It was perhaps the most notorious door in the Fleet, the personal office of the First Lord of the Fleet.

The door opened silently into the bulkhead.

"Enter," a man's voice called.

Marcelle stepped through first, moved to the right, and came to rest out of the way. Jessica followed an instant later.

As offices on fleet space stations went, it was neither large nor ostentatious, as befit the man sitting behind the desk. Two chairs in front, bolted down, a small plant in a pot on a sidebar, pictures of First Lord Kasum's father and brother in their full Senatorial regalia, scattered in with the pictures of the First Lord's wife and family. Behind him, a lovely oil painting of *RAN Devereux* against an orbital sunrise, back before the First Lord, or his first command, were famous.

Jessica stopped in front of the desk and waited. Some Fleet Lords demanded a salute, but First Lord Kasum had always been more about content than form, even back when he had been the Command Centurion instructing new recruits on fleet tactics at Fleet Boarding School, teaching a raw Scholarship Student how to maneuver in six axes of motion.

And he has not changed much in those eighteen years.

The hair was fully gray now. He was still thin as a rail, 1.83 meters tall and maybe 80 kilos soaking wet. The voice was the same rich bass, so incongruous coming from such an otherwise slender chest.

He fixed her with an appraising look for several seconds before turning his attention to her companion.

"Thank you, Marcelle," he said simply with a smile.

"First Lord," her steward murmured back.

Jessica couldn't look, but she would have been willing to bet the woman beside her was blushing furiously right now.

This from a woman who occasionally got so rowdy drunk they got thrown out of dockside dive bars. But who turned into an absolute kitten around members of the Fifty Families that ruled the *Republic of Aquitaine*.

"Travere," he continued, "I'm going to keep her here for a while. Kamil should be able to get you something to drink and a quiet spot to wait. Tell him I sent you, please."

"Aye, sir."

The door hissed shut a moment later.

Jessica studied her old instructor, her mentor, her guardian angel for several moments, but there were no clues to be had. His desk was completely bare save for an empty mug and a magnetic pen in its holder.

Finally, he smiled up at her and pointed at one of the chairs.

"Sit, Jessica."

She did.

The silence stretched.

"It was interesting," he finally began, "when I empaneled a Court for you. It had to be an even one, balanced between Fighting Lords and Noble Lords, but it also had to be a fair one. We are, after all, a Republic, not a democracy, so there is an expectation that the best will lead, out of a notion of service, rather than birthright."

He paused to study her face. She gave nothing away. It was a speech she had heard from him before.

"First Fleet Lord Loncar, after all, had charged you with something very serious. The Noble Lords do not take well to having their orders questioned, especially not so…publically."

Jessica kept her snarl to herself. Kasum was an ally, possibly even a friend, if she had had any of those at this point.

"I would expect to be punished, sir," she finally said into the hanging breech, "for doing my job poorly. For allowing a commanding Fleet Lord to establish an Order of Battle so poorly thought out. Not speaking up, not stopping him, would qualify."

Kasum waited, but she was done. This was his show. He nodded.

"So he put you on the right flank and ordered you to protect the carriers. Standard Fleet tactics, straight out of the manual, yes?"

"Correct," she replied, venom and disdain creeping into her voice. "With an unscouted moon outside the left flank."

"How many response maneuvers did you have plotted for your squadron, when the first Imperial fighters came around the horizon Jessica?"

She paused, not unsure of her answer, but unsure of her audience for the first time.

This man was one of the First Families. One of *Them*. How much could she safely tell him?

He nodded at her sudden discomfort, as if that alone answered the question. In a way, it had. He let the moment drag.

"Four," Jessica finally said, "with seventeen possible variants depending on the size and makeup of the attack."

She actually watched his eyes open wide.

It felt good to surprise him. She had rarely done it when she was a student.

He recovered in less than a blink.

"And if you had been in the position you practically demanded Loncar place you, at the start of the attack?"

She couldn't keep the sneer out of her voice this time, so she didn't try. "*Vigilant* probably would have required a week in drydock," she said harshly. "*Rubicon* less than that. My ship, *Brightoak*, perhaps nine to twelve days because we would have been the tip of the spear. As usual. Instead, *Brightoak* will be six to eight months having her nose rebuilt. *Rubicon* just flew again after five weeks. *Vigilant* might have to go to the wrecker, depending on how she's surveyed."

19

Jessica hadn't thought she could surprise her old tactics instructor twice in one meeting. It was one of those days.

Her anger felt hot and sudden in her belly, far more so that just facing a Court Martial.

"What makes you so sure, Jessica?" he asked quietly.

She took a deep breath to control her emotions, almost ashamed of him seeing her like this. Eighteen years seemed to slip away.

"Because it is standard Imperial flight technique, sir," she spit out, biting each word as it passed. "They would have flown into a wall of missiles, and then been trapped above us in the gravity well, trying to climb out of reach while we shot the hell out of them from below and two cruisers sat above and fired down on them. I believe your term, once upon a time, was mousetrap."

He smiled at her. "Okay, Provisional-Cornet Keller," he said, also falling back eighteen years, "how would you have handled the Order of Battle and why? Please show your work."

Jessica let go of a breathe she had not realized she was holding. The stress and heat seemed to flow out of her fingertips and ground into the cool wood of the desk. She smiled warmly for the first time today.

"I would have sent both wings of fighters under the southern pole hot and fast, with the destroyers right behind them, then the battlecruiser followed by the Fleet Carriers, with the two light cruisers in the rear providing flanking protection."

The First Lord cocked his head at her in wonder. "And what are the probabilities, cadet?"

She ticked them off on the desk with one hand. "First. If the patrol fighters are paying attention and are any good, they see us as soon as we clear the horizon, panic, and emergency scramble the wing. Considering that they had a supply tug modified to hold fighters and an older escort carrier, they can probably get ten fighters up by the time we arrive, so five to one odds, plus their carrier is outgunned by a factor of about fifty to one. Maybe they fight, maybe they strike. Depends on how stupid or crazy their commanding officer is."

"Second," she continued, tapping the desk in rhythm with her words. "They are not looking down like they should, and we get on top of them before they can do anything. Two patrol fighters facing fifty-four armed opponents, plus an enemy fleet, point blank. They strike immediately. We put crews aboard the Imperial vessels, ignore *Iger* completely, and fly home like rich pirates, laughing at them. Major tactical victory for us, possibly a significant strategic win across the entire sector, considering the loss of material resources on their side that have to then be replaced. They go on the defensive for at least a year."

He leaned back and watched her as she spoke.

Jessica blinked as she fell silent. It felt like squadron command school all over again. One of the Noble Lords would have probably just failed her out of his class for such reckless audacity.

Nils Kasum was a Fighting Lord. Had been one of the best of them.

"Very well analyzed, Cadet," he smiled at her. "When the fleet returned home, I had a group of friends game out the scenario at *Iger* over a case of wine. Most came to the same consensus you did. Two of them would have gone on and attacked *Iger* anyway."

Jessica pursed her lips, but refrained from commenting.

Kasum noticed and stopped.

"You disapprove, Jessica," he asked honestly. "You? One of my most aggressive destroyer squadron commanders? Why? Why not attack *Iger*, having stripped her defenses?"

"Pushing your luck, First Lord," she whispered. "A good commander knows when to take all the credits off the table and go home laughing. That one, last, seductive call of the dice is what breaks you. Every time."

His smile said something. She wasn't exactly sure. Perhaps she had just passed a test she didn't even know she was taking?

He leaned forward to rest his elbows on the desk and lace his fingers under his chin. She felt like a minnow facing a shark.

"What I'm about to tell you, Command Centurion Keller," he began formally, all the banter gone from his voice, "does not leave this room. Ever. Am I clear?"

Jessica nodded, suddenly understanding the little hints around her in the last month led here. The Court Martial. The media stories. The leaks to the press. The acquittal. Even the banter with her old mentor. She felt doors closing around her while she waited for him to open the one in front of her. "Aye, sir."

"It's very simple, Jessica. We're losing the war."

The whole universe slid out from under Jessica. The room grew cold. She felt her eyes grow a little, but quickly brought her face back under control. The hot fire of rage in her belly refused to settle, though.

"Losing, First Lord?" she asked, unable to regain her calmness. Her life had been dedicated to the war. Fighting it. Winning it.

"Losing," he said simply. "It isn't obvious, and won't be for a decade or more, but we are losing. Or rather, the Empire has a small tactical advantage and they have begun to push us back in a way that will accelerate slowly over time. It's only visible as a shadow on the largest pictures of the war front."

"I see," Jessica muttered.

"The thrust at *Iger* was intended to open a new front," Kasum said. "Drive a wedge into a major trade route. Force them onto the defensive for a few years so we could rebuild the fleet. Their advantage isn't much right now. Perhaps an extra cruiser laid down every year. But those things build up over time."

"How can I help, First Lord?" Jessica asked. She could feel her equilibrium slowly return.

"In here, right now, you can call me Nils, Jessica. I'm about to ask you to do something crazy, so I need us to be on a personal level, and not just a professional one."

"I see...Nils," she replied.

Just how crazy? Just how personal? Irrational thoughts flashed across her eyes. *Was he planning to marry her off to one of his relatives in some sort of political alliance? One of his enemies? Her? The Scholarship Student from a blue collar family?*

He was smiling at her discomfort, so it must not be too bad. *Right?*

Everything she was, everything she had become, was because of this man. From her earliest days as a raw cadet to the youngest-ever squadron commander in the *RAN*. He could reasonably ask for just about anything at his point. And she would find a way to make it happen. Happiness be damned.

"I'm intrigued by your comment on pirates, Jessica," he finally said.

She thought that anything he might have said would have been less confusing. *Pirates?*

"Pirates? Nils?"

"At *Iger*, you would have been happy capturing four squadrons of Imperial fighters and their crews, and a pair of past-their-prime ships, and running away. Other commanders likely would have destroyed everything out of hand, or gambled on attacking *Iger* afterwards."

"That's right." Jessica had no idea where this line of questioning was going. She was an expert on fleet maneuvers, not political ones.

"Right now, I cannot throw another fleet together and make another attempt like *Iger*, anywhere along the war frontier," Nils said, tapping his finger on the desk.

With a start, Jessica realized where she had picked up the habit. At least she had emulated the best.

"The two sides will both be recovering for a year," he said.

"What can I do?" Jessica asked simply.

"I want you to think like a pirate," came the response.

Jessica felt an eyebrow try to climb off of the top of her head. Pirate? Her? Silence seemed the best course of action right now.

"You are too much of a distraction for the fleet right now, Jessica. Have you been following the media?"

"Yes, sir. Nils." She just could not fathom either the hero worship nor the vitriol her case had sparked. Was she that far out of touch with ordinary people?

"I want to send you someplace quiet for a time, away from the limelight," he continued. "And turn you loose to act like a pirate."

"I...see."

"Your squadron will have to make a lot of noise and distract the *Fribourg Empire*, much like we were trying to do at *Iger*, but you won't have the resources necessary to invade anywhere or hold enemy systems. I want you on the tactical and strategic offensive, and knock them onto their heels for a while."

"That's all well and good, Nils, but *Brightoak* won't be ready for battle for at least a year."

"I'm aware of that, Jessica," he said. "You won't be taking that squadron with you."

"No? What will I be using, First Lord?"

She just couldn't keep calling this man by his given name. It felt so awkward.

"Jessica, the Court of Inquiry struck all charges, and further, they recommended your team for a unit citation and you for a medal. As First Lord, it is in my prerogative to also reward you in a different way."

She watched him open a desk drawer, dread warring with savage glee as he pulled out a familiar-looking official document, signed it, and slid it across the desk at her.

'By will of the Republic of Aquitaine Navy and First Lord Nils Kasum, the undersigned, Command Centurion Jessica Keller, is hereby ordered to...'

She quickly read through the document, noting the space at the bottom for her to sign in front of her new crew on the new ship when she took command.

She read it again and looked up at him. "I'm not familiar with this ship, sir."

"She is an older vessel, Jessica," he said with a warm smile. "Currently relegated to a quiet frontier sector where she mostly patrols to keep pirates at bay. The fleet occasionally rotates ships and crews through the area when they've been at the tip of the spear too long. The *Fribourg Empire* does the same, across the wide, black gulf between them. I want you to set that part of the border on fire, to make the *Empire* have to spend a lot of time and ships and people stopping you, when they might be better spent stopping me somewhere else."

"And how do you propose I do that?" she asked. "Which Fleet Lord will I be answering to?"

"Myself," he smiled triumphantly. "This ship is already something of an unofficial flag ship for the sector forces, and there is no Fleet Lord currently assigned. That means the only person giving you orders is me."

Jessica smiled like a schoolgirl. Or a shark.

She read the name of the ship again. It sounded fierce.

RAN Auberon.

CHAPTER VII

Date of the Republic July 2, 392 Anameleck Prime

The sound as the ground vehicle settled to a halt perked up Bogdan Loncar from his fugue.

A doorman in a muted uniform sprang into action and had the rear door open almost before the vehicle stopped.

"Fleet Lord Loncar," he said with a deep and sincere bow, "allow me to welcome you to the Club this evening."

Bogdan glanced briefly at the man as he exited. "Good evening, Johnathon."

The doorman, Johnathon, quickly closed the vehicle door and stepped to the imposing wooden door to the Club. He swung the heavy portal open on massive hinges and gestured Loncar to enter.

Bogdan took a few moments to let his eyes adjust to the dimness as Johnathon closed the vault-like door behind him, cutting off the outside world. The entry smelled vaguely of rich tobacco and warm chocolate, friendly smells trapped in the weave of the lush rug and the tapestried walls.

He glanced to his right and noted the Guardian of the Inner Chamber, the Concierge, patiently awaiting him.

"Matthias," Bogdan nodded.

The man nodded back. "Fleet Lord Tesar has left a message that he would welcome your company this evening. Last I checked, he was just about to order dinner in the Rockery on the third floor."

"Very good, Matthias," the Fleet Lord replied. "Is Samantha available this evening?"

"She is, sir," the man smiled. "I will have her deliver your drinks immediately."

"Thank you, Matthias."

Bogdan stepped deeper into the dimly-lit hallway and climbed the grand staircase. Starships didn't have elevators, so a proper club that served current and retired naval officers did not either.

Tonight, an elevator might have been more pleasant. Bogdan grumbled to himself as he climbed the stairs, his old knees and back complaining. It had not been a good week.

Upstairs, he passed a variety of men, and a few women, all well dressed, well bred. Proper representatives of the founding Families of the *Republic*. His class of people.

The staff was also proper. Polite, cheerful, discrete, knowledgeable. He could leave his worries and cares outside and relax here, safe.

It was just another reason to stay a day's sail away from the Capital, *Ladaux*, and all that political mess. *Anameleck Prime* was old money, old industry. It had been one of the first worlds of the future *Republic* to return to space flight after the long darkness when the Homeworld was destroyed, thousands of years ago.

On the third floor, Bogdan made his way past several doorways and side halls. He entered a large door at the end and looked around. The room was large, but broken into a variety of small nooks and cubbyholes by careful use of short walls, plants, and pillars.

"Good evening, Lord Loncar," a young woman purred as she approached, a brandy snifter on a tray in one hand.

"Good evening, Samantha," he replied with a polite leer. At his age, he was too old to engage in bedroom gymnastics, but he did appreciate having a beautiful young woman to ogle while doing business. Especially a short brunette with long hair, lush curves, and a ripe bosom. One who understood that the business of Navy men was serious work and that they needed to escape their daily responsibilities occasionally.

"Lord Tesar is this way, sir," She said, leading him deeper into the room, to a particularly private corner table.

"Evening, Bogdan," boomed a voice as he approached.

"Bogusław," he replied, feeling the weight of the day slide off his shoulders as the lovely woman disappeared back into the room.

Bogusław Tesar was a decade older, and had been retired from the Fleet for longer than that. He had begun to go to seed in the way that a previously-active man will when they stop working so hard. He was thick around the middle, but in a stout way. His hair had finally turned completely white after he had stopped coloring it. The shoulders had developed a slouch.

He looked like a man getting ready to die of old age.

"Heard the news," Tesar said gravely. "Looks like Kasum won this round?"

"Perhaps," Bogdan said. "Perhaps not. That little minx got away scot free, but I understand that the First Lord is sending her to the *Cahllepp Frontier* instead of back to the main front."

"Interesting." Tesar took a deep swig of something caramel-colored with a lot of ice. "Do you suppose she was broken by the experience, after all? Or maybe Kasum has lost his confidence in her? Either way, it removes one of his important pieces from the table."

"I believe it is the latter," Bogdan said, taking a drink of his own. Samantha always knew how to get them made to exact specifications, regardless of the bartender on duty.

"I do know that a number of Fleet Lords have expressed concern about having her serve under them, after her antics at *Iger*. Perhaps she has worn out her welcome."

Samantha returned at that moment with a menu for him and interrupted their conversation with service and hints of cleavage.

This was beginning to feel like a victory dinner.

Bogdan leaned back as Samantha cleared their plates from the table and delivered a fresh round of brandy.

As she departed, both men took a long moment to appreciate the architecture of her construction. It was a very fine ass.

"So, Bogdan," Tesar said in a conspiratorial tone, "what's next for you? Back to the fleet, or will you finally stand for office?"

"I plan to return to duty soon, Bogusław," he growled back. "Kasum has decided to blame me for *Iger*, but I have too much seniority to be kept shorebound for long. In time, the other Noble Lords will agitate enough and he will be forced to return me to command. If we have to engineer for a new First Lord before that can to happen, I am willing to entertain that notion."

"Oh? Who do you think we might contact, if we needed to create such a dramatic change at the top?"

Bogdan smiled and leaned forward. "Well, first…"

CHAPTER VIII

Date of the Republic October 1, 392 Kismayo system

Jessica looked up suddenly as Marcelle touched her knee. Apparently, she'd been lost in her notes and reading for two hours. Docking must be imminent.

Sure enough, the monitor on the shuttle's bulkhead showed a sleek gray warship sitting against the black background, like a great whale breeching on a calm sea. It swelled very slowly as she approached. They would be aboard in a few minutes.

Jessica nodded to Marcelle and began stowing devices and papers in her travel satchel. Everything there was to know about the Strike Carrier *RAN Auberon* and her crew. Specifically her crew. They had been stuck out here in a quiet corner for a long time.

She glanced at the prep sheet Marcelle had prepared for her. Thumbnail pictures of the department heads and key officers, so she could remember names and faces them. The two of them had spent long hours memorizing them.

Jessica was firmly convinced that there was nothing worse than serving under a Command Centurion who took weeks to learn his officer's names. It was lazy, the mark of someone who was here because he was well-connected and on his way to serve in the Republic Senate or some other political job.

At the dawn of civilization, the Romans had reputedly made people like that Tribunes without putting them in direct command.

Jessica thought the Fleet could learn something useful from the Roman practice. Especially here.

Auberon's former Commander hadn't even waited for her to arrive with her orders to replace him. As soon as he had learned he was being transferred, he had turned over command to his Executive Officer, boarded a shuttle, and disappeared.

Jessica smiled. Augustine Kwok was a nephew by marriage of Fleet Lord Loncar, so it did save everyone some level of awkwardness for him to not be there to formally turn over command. It was obviously intended to be a snub to her, and was certainly rude, but well within the letter of regulations, if not the spirit.

And he had been in command out here for a little more than three years. He must have done something especially stupid back home for that kind of exile.

How had the crew responded to being under command of one of the scions of the Fifty Families for so long…?

She was just about to find out.

Jessica handed Marcelle a stack of old-fashioned linen envelopes, hand-written with names on them and numbered. This crew was due for a surprise shortly. How well they took it would determine just how ugly things were going to get on both side of the frontier.

She had a war to win.

Jessica waited inside the shuttle's crew bay on *Auberon's* Flight Deck. Marcelle had already exited with both satchels, leaving her alone in the poorly-lit metal box.

Jessica took a deep breath, glanced down at the scroll of paper she held in one hand, and finished counting to one hundred.

She emerged from the hatch and looked out over the cavernous bay.

Strike Carriers were purpose-built vessels, redesigned up from a heavy cruiser hull. As carriers went, they were considered tiny and cramped. But they still had to be large enough to hold and fly three sections of fighters, nine craft, plus the standard three transport shuttles from the cruiser design. In this case, the design had been made even tighter by removing the three shuttles and replacing them with two larger craft, a gunship and an assault shuttle.

Still, it was considered a courtesy to a new commanding officer to be met with an empty flight deck. Jessica had heard stories of carriers where the full wing had been launched in order to leave the entirety of the deck available.

That was extravagance that was normally reserved for Fleet Lords taking command of the big Fleet Carriers, in ceremonies that might last days.

Jessica suppressed a smile as she emerged into the bright lights of her new Flight Deck. Everything had been shifted back into storage cradles to make space, except for one fighter craft that sat to one side, looking as if it was ready to launch. Most of *Auberon's* officers were lined up across from it, facing it, making an aisle for her to walk down, as if on parade.

So much for the expectation of a cleared deck. The regulations did say clean, but nothing required everything to be packed up and stowed.

Again, within the letter of the regulations, but extremely irregular and possibly bordering on rude.

Jessica had been afraid that three years under a commander she knew to be a sanctimonious and pompous windbag might have damaged the crew's morale.

She was wrong. This was a crew with spirit.

She could work with that.

They might hate her, but they were all volunteers, and exhibited, even according to Kwok's records, competence that occasionally bordered on excellence.

Jessica stepped down onto the deck and entered the parade aisle they had made for her, radiating grim seriousness.

Inside, she fought not to smile. This crew was looking for a fight with her.

While Jessica was a warrior, she was also a tactician. She began adjusting her plans.

Jessica came to a stop in front of the man at the far end of the line on her right, pivoted, and took a moment to scan him closely. He had two stripes on his arm for a Senior Centurion, and the look of a quietly competent man.

The pictures Marcelle had supplied had not done the man justice. He was average height and average build. Average looking, with red/auburn hair that was stronger than she had expected.

Denis Jež had a record that showed him to be smart but not brilliant. Methodical. Exceptionally competent. He was also, according to the records, a chess player. Jessica could not imagine someone less like her.

But he also had a record of serving under more senior commanders who had a tendency towards political connections. According to the First Lord, Denis had been assigned to make sure Kwok didn't do anything embarrassing.

Jessica assumed he was a babysitter, who was probably quietly distraught that he had not been considered for command. Jessica softened her scowl, watched his own relax. Jež did not have a powerful and important family or patron to advance his career.

But she didn't plan on being out here in the boonies forever. She hoped to find a place for him in her greater schemes.

"Centurion Jež?" she said formally, waiting for him to nod.

She opened the scroll, took a step back, and projected her voice loud enough to be heard by the back ranks.

'By will of the Republic of Aquitaine Navy and First Lord Nils Kasum, the undersigned, Command Centurion Jessica Keller, is hereby ordered to report aboard the RAN Auberon at the earliest opportunity and take command, subject to the normal rules and regulations. She will exercise excellence and demand the same of her crew, that the whole reflect the greatest acclaim in serving the needs of the Republic and the will of the Senate.

Signed on the Date of The Republic June 26, 392 by First Lord Nils Kasum and countersigned October 1, 392 by Jessica Keller.'

Jessica looked up at the crew briefly, watched some of the tension bleed out of Centurion Jež's face, and pulled a pen from a pocket in her tunic. She quickly signed the document, scrolled it, and handed it to her new First Officer.

"Centurion," Jessica said formally, "I relieve you."

"I stand relieved," he replied quietly as he took the document.

Jessica turned to the other officers before her. This crew tended to be younger than one would expect for a frontier posting, but Kasum had told her that Auberon was the unofficial flagship of the sector, and appeared to be crewed by a higher grade of personnel, competent instead of well-connected.

She allowed herself to smile at them, watching the faces relax somewhat from the apprehension of the unknown.

She fixed Jež with a sharp eye. To his credit, the man did not squirm.

"Jež," she said, loud enough to be heard several rows back. "In one word, what is the status of *Auberon* for combat operations?"

The man blinked once, a poker player suddenly keeping his cards close to the vest. "Ready."

"Good enough for now, Centurion Jež," she replied.

"Ma'am?" he said, confused enough to break character for the first time. The other officers also began to look less solemn, like perhaps this wasn't going to be an execution, after all. Or maybe it was.

"The correct answer is *hungry*," she announced loudly. "This is a warship of the *Republic of Aquitaine*, ladies and gentlemen. We are about to go to war."

Jessica didn't wait for the crew to respond.

She nodded to Marcelle, who walked up and handed her the stack of envelopes.

Jessica considered them closely for a second. Hand-written notes, personally addressed to a number of officers. Right now, their hatred of her would probably start. By tomorrow, perhaps, grudging admiration. Eventually, they would achieve excellence.

Senior Centurion Denis Jež winced to himself as he watched the new commander review the crew, and then winced when he saw that stack of envelopes. Commander Keller was not reacting in a way like any new commander he had ever served under.

The crew's behavior, and how they'd set up her arrival ceremony might have been a mistake. It had been a calculated gamble on their part, based on this woman's reputation.

He had heard the stories about her. They all had.

One of the youngest-ever destroyer commanders in Fleet history. The youngest-ever destroyer squadron commander. A commoner, like him, another of the *Scholarship Students* found by talent scouts and groomed for the Fleet.

Up close, it was hard to identify what it was about her that left him so unsettled. She was shorter than he expected, but at the same time exuded a size and energy of someone much taller and much bigger. She seemed to fill the hangar bay with her presence.

And yet, for all that energy, she moved with a spare precision, almost like a training robot. Not a wasted motion. Not a step out of place.

If one could chain a hurricane, perhaps harness it and unleash it on command, it would have that feeling about it. Like lightning about to strike. Denis sniffed silently for a hint of ozone.

Some officers were boringly predictable, by-the-book types. They could be endured if needed, driven mad carefully if necessary, if one stayed exactly within regulations. Those rarely came out to this frontier, anyway.

Other officers, generally the well-born, just wanted to serve out their time in the remote distance from the capital worlds, either hiding from some scandal until things blew over, or punching a safe dance card on their way to important elective office. Command Centurion Kwok, the recently-departed, and not-much-respected commander, fell into that latter category.

Jež had served with both kinds. This new one, Command Centurion Jessica Keller, frightened him in ways he could not name. And the look she gave him, gave all of them, did not promise sunshine and happiness.

Whatever moment had come for all of them passed. He watched her flip a switch in her mind. She suddenly seemed to be moving at a higher plane than the rest of them. Swimming in air while they floundered in quicksand.

It was the beginning of the future, for all of them.

He watched her turn back to study the Starfighter on the deck behind her. The M-5 *Harpoon* melee fighters were old, but well maintained. The ones on *Auberon* were often older than their pilots. Newer ordinance went to the combat frontiers.

She studied the craft for a few moments. Technically, it could be construed as an insult to a new commander to have it there, although nothing in the regulations forbid it. Pushing the limits was something a crew might do to test a new commander. Especially one with a reputation like Keller's.

She turned back and studied the crowd before her, silently for several seconds, until she apparently found the face she wanted, standing in back.

"Flight Centurion Darya Lagunov," she smiled at the woman. "Since you seem to have drawn the short straw today, could you join me please?"

Denis glanced briefly over his shoulder. She knew Lagunov by sight? Had she memorized the whole crew? He knew the two women had never served together. *Bitter Kitten* had come to *Auberon* straight out of advanced flight training.

Then he looked closely at the M-5 fighter. It was pointed to the left, so the only name visible on the cockpit was Darya's callsign nickname, *Bitter Kitten*, painted on it.

Had this new commander memorized those as well?

An equally puzzled Flight Centurion broke ranks and emerged. She crossed the small space and saluted. Denis watched Keller return the salute and direct the pilot to stand next to her, facing the rest of the crew.

This welcome ceremony had definitely gone very, very far off script.

"I had considered," Keller began, booming such a big sound from such a small woman, "taking it easy for a few days. Getting to know all of you a little more personally before we dove into our next mission. This is a new ship and a new crew for me, after all. Some commanders like to ease into things, to give everyone a chance to know each other better."

Denis could imagine the shocked looks on the faces beside and behind him. They were just now waking up to what this woman, this Command Centurion Jessica Keller, represented. They were used to Command Centurion Kwok, who did everything by the books.

Denis could hear the intakes of breath, or hisses depending.

They had apparently tugged on a tiger's tail.

"In fact," he heard her continue in that same booming voice that sounded so conversational, "I plan to add a suggestion box in Hallway Four, near Engineering, just so people can make suggestions, signed or anonymous, on how things could be done better. You are a good crew, you should have good ideas."

Her voice was a high alto, pitched just right for the room. Denis had heard others with that timbre. It was a learned skill that good commanders mastered.

"You shouldn't think of it as a doubloon nailed to main mast, people. I want to know how we can be the best."

"Because," she continued, "I believe we are ready to face confrontation and danger together right now. We are ready to prove to Fleet Command that *Auberon* is worthy of their trust in us."

Denis watched her fan out the stack of envelops in her hand and study them for a moment. He took a deep breath that mirrored hers.

"With that in mind," she said firmly, "I am declaring a training exercise, ship-wide, beginning now. First Officer Jež and I have been assassinated. The assassin has been killed. Tactical Centurion Strnad, you are in command until the exercise is completed."

Denis almost relaxed. Almost. This would be a test for what had been his crew, and would reflect on him as a trainer and leader, but there was nothing to do now but watch. And learn. There were many things to learn from watching this woman, this whirlwind.

Nothing he had read about her had prepared him for what she was like in person.

Senior Centurion Strnad blinked once, possibly, and then came to rigid attention. She was a big woman, almost 1.9 meters, but built at a perfectly normal ratio for someone an entire head shorter. It was only up close that her scale became apparent. Her black hair bobbed as she looked down at her approaching commander.

He watched Keller walk to the woman to his immediate left and hand her four envelopes. Glancing down, he could see they were numbered. *Just how detailed was her planning?*

"I will observe, and occasionally offer advice, or information that you would normally have access to, if you were to open my safe or Jež's, and read the contents. Since that is not necessary, we will remain as scorekeepers for now."

Denis watched as Keller moved down the line several bodies to stand in front of one of the officers he would not have expected to be singled out. She smiled at the man who looked surprised.

"Commander Strnad, my orders, as contained in your envelope #1, were to rendezvous with the rest of our squadron. You will make Junior Centurion Zivkovic your Flag Centurion for the remainder of this exercise."

Denis couldn't tell who was the more surprised of the three. Zivkovic was a brilliant young officer, but had come from a very poor family. Both men were Scholarship Students, which, upon reflection, covered about half of the officers here, including the commander. Was that what Keller was testing?

"Commander Strnad," Jessica continued, "you will now read your orders. I will let you know which envelope to open next when it is appropriate."

Denis watched his second officer slide a finger under a seam to open it. *Was that wax?*

She pulled out a piece of heavy paper and unfolded it. Denis caught a glance of spidery handwriting written in bright blue ink.

A few moments passed, hushed, incipient.

Tamara Strnad looked up at her new Command Centurion and fixed her with a hard stare for a moment. Denis watched Keller nod briefly, warmly, encouragingly.

Maybe, just maybe, they hadn't completely pissed off their new commander on her first day.

"All hands," Strnad called loudly. She didn't have the tone or cadence of Keller's voice, but it carried to the assembled crew. "Bring the ship to active alert. Primary command officers to the bridge."

Strnad pulled out a smaller envelope and handed it to *Auberon's* Pilot, her hands only shaking a little as she did so.

"Centurion Zupan, you will bring the engines to ninety-five percent and plot a minimum time course to these coordinates. We will make the transition to Jumpspace from there."

Strnad turned to look back at the Flight Deck crew, three rows behind her. "Clear the flight deck and prepare for combat launches. You have at least ninety-six hours before we engage. Prepare accordingly. Move it people. The clock is running!"

Denis felt an almost out-of-body experience watching the crew suddenly break formation and sprint to their stations.

Auberon had just jumped feet first into the war.

CHAPTER IX

Date of the Republic October 1, 392 Kismayo system

The lightning was there. Jessica felt a twinge race down her spine.

It was a huge gamble, unleashing the crew like this. It would be easy to break them, break their morale, shatter their comradery doing this.

It was also the fastest way to weld them together into a weapon, to fashion *Auberon* as a saber for her left hand.

What she intended to do, Jessica required far more than just an able crew. And she didn't have three years to work them up to the level she needed.

The First Lord had said it many times over the years. "Risk equals reward." Or, as she privately thought of it, "Live by the sword…"

Jessica frequently lived by the sword.

She snagged *Bitter Kitten* by the sleeve as the woman started to join her mates.

The pilot gave her a shocked look, partly for the physical contact, partly because her new commander was apparently much stronger than she looked.

Jessica smiled up at her.

"Lagunov," she said quietly as the storm erupted around them, "You are also a casualty for now. I would appreciate if you could accompany me to the bridge with Centurion Jež, and then join us for dinner later when everyone settles down."

Jessica watched the shocked look grow, peak, and then recede.

"Aye, sir," she whispered back.

"Good," Jessica said. "The mob should be about cleared out. Let's join them."

Jessica watched the slowest members of the crew finish racing up the broad staircase to the main deck. She paused to make sure she had two followers behind her, three with Marcelle, and fell into the wake.

The bridge was in a state of nervous energy when she arrived, as the junior officers who had been manning everything during the ceremony below were bumped from their chairs and replaced by senior staff. Most remained, tucking themselves into corners, training stations, or finding a section of wall to occupy quietly.

Jessica slid next to one such crewman, a young man with the single broken stripe of a Cornet on his sleeve.

There was a momentary look of utter horror crossed his face as he realized the person he had just accidentally bumped into was his new commanding officer.

She smiled and gestured for him to stay put.

Marcelle had taken up a station by the main hatch, next to the security marine, where she could easily escape the bridge to run errands as needed. Always planning ahead.

Lagunov had ended up next to Jessica, with Jež just beyond. Even better.

She and her First Officer, her Exec, could talk about the exercise in front of the pilot, and the whole conversation would be reported ship-wide within a day. It would be far easier than having meetings to brief everyone.

Jessica studied the bridge for a few moments. It was much longer than *Brightoak's* had been, as befit a larger vessel with a small flight wing, and held about twice as many people normally, doubled again with the training exercise underway.

The bubbling noise was growing as people whispered to their mates, and the filtration system kicked on to deal with the sudden crush of bodies and the smell of excitement.

Tamara Strnad had settled into the central chair. She looked around for a moment at the mess and found Jessica over her left shoulder. She gave Jessica a look to ask a silent question.

Jessica smiled back and nodded as if to say *It's your bridge. Go ahead.*

Strnad took a deep breath while Jessica watched.

Jessica understood. She had been in that chair a number of times during these kinds of training scenarios, once with the man who would be First Lord watching.

"Everyone who was on duty," Tamara called loudly over the din, "if you just got bumped, you can retire to the Emergency Bridge and watch, or go catch up on sleep or paperwork. Senior crew will fill the rest of this shift and then cover their normal one. Someone call the wardroom and ask them to fire up the brew pots."

The noise surged for a moment, only to be silenced by Strnad's harsh call of, "Now," cutting across them.

Jessica watched the bridge empty as if someone had pulled a plug. The junior Cornet standing next to her started to leave, but she pointed to him and then to a training station nearby.

"Sit. Watch. Learn," she said quietly.

The man goggled at her for a moment, and then rushed to sit down.

Strnad watched it play out and nodded, before she turned back to the men and women in front of her.

"Engineering. Status?" she called.

Jessica was impressed. For all the obvious adrenalin in her system, Tamara sounded like a commander. It was not always an easy thing to do.

Auberon's Engineer had always struck Jessica as amusing, reading his file. Vilis Ozolinsh was short, broad, and ethnically Mongolian, but sounded like the bluest of blue bloods from the Fifty Families. He was from one of the noblest clans, but had fallen in love with jumpdrives at an early age and never looked back.

He looked up from his complex board and turned to the Pilot without looking at the central chair. "Power is currently at eighty-four percent and climbing. Reactors stable within normal parameters. We are prepared for maximum effort at any time you desire."

Strnad nodded. "Navigation. Status?"

The Pilot's fingers danced across her complex flight board like a concert pianist playing a recital. She smiled, lighting up an otherwise plain and somewhat homely face. Her long blond ponytail bobbed in time to some inner rhythm.

"Two course options available, Commander," she said. "Straight shot out will take us about four hours to reach the jump. Or we can dive into the gravity well, slingshot once around the planet, and shave about thirty minutes off our ETA. Downside, it will make life hell for the shuttle pilot, once she drops her cargo and wants to get back to the surface. Orders?"

Jessica watched Tamara weigh the options in her head for a second. Tamara turned to look at her for a second. Jessica shrugged.

"Go for the slingshot, Zupan," she called. "Better a minute early than a minute late."

Jessica smiled. That was the unofficial motto of the Fleet, whispered to each other while racing between classes.

The pianist smiled and began a silent concerto on her desktop.

Jessica always thought that her inner ear felt the shifts as a big vessel turned, even though scientists had long since concluded that the effects of the gravplates created an inertial field around a vessel like a bubble. Tea she was drinking in a mug might not ripple, but her ear knew.

From her corner, Jessica watched Strnad eye the three remaining envelopes briefly, speculatively, before tucking them down the side of her chair by her leg.

When she opened those, that was where it would get interesting.

CHAPTER X

Date of the Republic October 1, 392 Kismayo system

It was the last of the tea.

Tamara emptied the last dregs in her mug and locked it back into the holder. She had already gone to pee once, an hour ago. It would look bad to go again so soon. Adrenalin was an utter bitch, especially when you had a commander with a rep like Keller's.

Tamara scanned the bridge, taking in the commander, the XO, and the fighter pilot huddled in one corner. The whispers were too quiet to hear over the air system, so she could only guess what was being said. Hopefully, she hadn't looked too bad on her first day with the new boss.

She checked her readouts again to be sure, and the spoke up. It was unlikely that there was anybody on the bridge without a little countdown clock on their screen, but just in case…

"Navigation. Time to jump coordinates?" she called.

She watched Nada Zupan, the Pilot, come out of a fugue like a swimmer surfacing. The long blond ponytail snapped once as her head shivered.

"ETA fourteen minutes, sir," she replied, quiet, intent. "We'll actually be far enough clear of the gravity well in six that we could crash jump, if we had to."

"Hmmm. Ozolinsh," Tamara continued, "what would happen if we had to jump right now?"

The Engineer looked over a shoulder at her as if she had asked him to sacrifice his first born.

"We'd probably be able to get about twelve or fifteen light hours out before the calibrations came apart and we spent a day fixing everything," he growled. "In seven minutes, the calibrations can be redone inline, and tweaked when we come out the other side. In fifteen, you won't notice we've transitioned."

"Roger that," Tamara replied with a smile. Her orders had simply said to take command and bring the ship to this point before awaiting further orders. And she still had three envelopes left.

Tamara suppressed a shiver at what might be in them.

Oh, what the hell.

She pulled the three out. Each had a number hand-written on the outside. 2. 3. 4.

Tamara turned to look over her shoulder. Command Centurion Keller stared back, a hard and unreadable look on her face.

Tamara held up the three envelopes and looked a question Keller, comfortably seated in the corner.

She was rewarded by the commander holding up three fingers.

Tamara cracked open the wax seal and pulled out the paper inside to read.

Oh, my.

She called up a navigation gazetteer and cycled through planetary systems until she found the one she wanted.

Yes. That's what I thought. More adventures for the crew. Wonder if I'll still be in charge for that? Might be fun. Might totally suck.

She pressed a button her screen.

"Navigation," she called, loud enough to wake everyone up from any daydreams that might have intruded. "I'm sending you coordinates for the far edge of the *Simeon* system. Lay them in and prepare to jump."

Tamara took a deep breath, aware she was showing off, but understanding that she needed to right now. Command Centurion Keller had a reputation as a brilliant tactical officer, but also a good commander who took the words of the command orders seriously, to "*exercise excellence and demand the same of her crew.*"

"Engineering," Tamara continued, "Gazetteer says eighty hours to *Simeon* for a well-founded ship. What's your estimate?"

Ozolinsh fixed her with his best withering stink-eye. "When we jump in eleven minutes," he replied firmly, not willing to give an inch on damaging his engines without a fight, "Seventy-two hours. If you jump in six minutes, seventy-seven. Your choice."

Tamara fought down the smile. Needling the man was fun, but inappropriate now that she was the commander. She understood suddenly why Keller looked so harsh.

She was never off duty.

Will I grow up to be like that?

Tamara thought about it for a second.

Do I want to be that successful? That respected?

Yes.

She started to work on what she considered her Command Scowl. Hopefully she would get more chances to use it.

"All right," she said suddenly, thumbing a button to bring the Flight Deck into the conversation. "Department heads, please rearrange your schedules to have senior staff come on duty in roughly seventy hours. As you may remember, *Simeon* is a naval weapon's range, and we will be exercising bangs and booms when we get there. Flight Deck, we'll discuss weapons load-out tomorrow and then plan sortie schedules."

Tamara watched a scrolling marquee message appear on her board from the Flight Deck Commander. *"Roger that. Iskra,"* was repeated until she pushed a button to acknowledge it.

They hadn't been nearly as surprised down on the flight deck as the looks and gasps on the bridge had been.

Tamara smiled. *Auberon* really was going to war.

CHAPTER XI

She considered belching.

That had been an utterly amazing shrimp and spinach risotto, followed by a tiramisu that was divine. Jessica watched the Wardroom's Chief Steward remove the last dessert plates from in front of her, *Bitter Kitten*, and Denis Jež before he refilled mugs and disappeared.

She smiled. Someone had taken the time to research the new Command Centurion in far greater depth and detail than the command staff had thought to do. It was too bad that it was her new chef.

Then again, maybe not.

Her mug of coffee was even the right roast. Who said life on the frontier had to be all deprivation?

"So, Lagunov," Jessica began, "how ready is the flight wing going to be?"

Pilots, by their nature, tended to be cocky, arrogant, and full of themselves. *Bitter Kitten* was none of that, as six hours of close contact had revealed. Instead, she was a skinny brunette of average height who spoke with quiet care and precision instead of bravado and bluster. Jessica wasn't sure what to make of her.

"Sharp," she replied, "but not too sharp. Commander Kwok had us the range at *Simeon* every six or eight months. Plus regular piracy patrols."

"Ever catch any?" Jessica asked, looking at both the pilot and her new Executive Officer, deep in his own mug of tea.

Bitter Kitten shrugged and sipped at a glass of port. "Rarely. Kwok would come out at a safe distance, launch the birds, and then let us chase them. Usually, they had enough time to get away. We were rarely cleared to launch the kind of missiles that could run them down and scrag them before they could jump."

"So," Jessica turned to Jež, "standard fleet carrier tactics?"

He shrugged in turn. "The commander was very by-the-book on those sorts of things. Plus he was…well-bred."

Jessica nodded. "One of the Noble Lords, rather than a Fighting Lord?"

"One could phrase it that way, commander," he replied diplomatically.

Jessica took a drink to let the air simmer. She nodded to herself and fixed each of them with a look of irritation.

"I imagine things will be changing significantly around here, then. Jež, Lagunov, our orders are to rattle cages out here in the hinterlands. To do that, we're going to have to act like a warship in a warzone, and not an oversized Revenue Cutter on patrol. Everything I've heard about this ship suggests she could be among the best in the fleet, so I'm going to work the rest of you almost as hard as I work myself, and see what we can become. Questions?"

"Am I allowed to gossip about what I've heard, commander?" *Bitter Kitten* murmured.

Jessica's smile lit up. "Absolutely. I asked you here so I could pick your brain and see things that would not necessarily bubble up from the lower decks. A lot of Command Centurions say they have an open door. Few of them actually exercise it. Just remember that you'll be signing your name when you walk through that door. Most of the time, we will outrun the news of what we're doing."

"Understood, sir," the pilot nodded at her. She pushed back from the table with an accidental burp. "Excuse me. Since I'm off duty for a while, I'm going to go sleep for twelve hours. That food was lovely, sir. Thank you."

Jessica watched her stick her head into the kitchen to thank the staff before disappearing into the hallway.

She turned to see Jež giving her a strange look. "Yes?"

"Nothing," he said after a moment.

"Ask now," she replied, "when we leave here, you'll be scoring the exercise and preparing to turn back into the Executive Officer."

"Are you really as hard and tough and good as they say?"

Jessica blinked. Well, she had asked for it.

She fixed him with a stern look. He didn't blush or blink. Good.

"Yes," she said simply. "Denis, I believe I could win this war if given the chance. Not just push the *Fribourgers* back to where they started, but actually design the strategies and logistics to defeat them. First Lord sent me out here to start a war. In his words, to set the frontier on fire and make them dedicate whole fleets and committees to stopping me."

She took a sip and gauged his reaction.

He nodded back at her.

So far, so good.

"*Auberon* is a tool. The Flight Wing is a tool. This crew is a tool. They are all good ones, and you don't blunt a saber by mashing it against a rock. However, they *are* tools. They will get honed by use. Sharpened. Probably dinged and dented. Because we are going to go do something nobody has ever imagined. This little strike carrier is going to frighten entire fleets of Imperial ships. I would like to camp in orbit about *St. Legier* and say hello, one of these days."

She stopped to take a breath. Denis nodded at her.

"How can I serve?" he asked simply.

Jessica flashed to the notes in his personnel file. Loyal subordinate. Had served under several Command Centurions generally promoted for political reasons rather than command acumen, so he could be trusted to keep things in motion. Smart but not brilliant in the way of some of his subordinate officers. Nobody back at *Ladaux* interested in advancing his career. No great options, until he had the luck to be serving under her.

"Denis, this is going to be much bigger than *Auberon*. That you will see shortly. I'm going to be far too busy commanding a squadron to be engaged in the day-to-day operations of things here, although I will most assuredly be reading your reports much closer than Kwok ever did. Your job will be to keep everything and everybody on an even keel. When we go into combat, and we will, you will be commanding *Auberon* at the tactical level while I handle strategy. I know you can do that, and do it very well. Keep that up and we will have the opportunity to do great things together. Good enough?"

She watched his eyes as he processed. According to the file, he was also a chess player, and pretty good. Jessica was a fencer. It was an entirely different way to think and move, but he would complement her well, if she could rely on him. What she needed was to know if he had that spark left, after being a babysitter for so long.

"Aye, sir," he finally said. "We'll give them hell."
She shook his outstretched hand. So far, so good.

CHAPTER XII

In some ways, it was an entirely new sound, but not anything unique when she thought about it. Jessica stood quietly in a side hallway with the door opened and listened to the Flight Deck Commander call the roll.

Iskra Vlahovic was a rare bird in the fleet. She had been a pilot until she'd been shot up enough that she couldn't fly combat missions any more. Instead of retiring to a desk job or piloting shuttles, she had gone back and gotten advanced degrees in engineering and eventually taken command of the flight deck of *Auberon*.

If she couldn't fly, according to the information in her personnel file, at least she was keep others going.

From the discipline records, the woman ran a tight ship. Infractions were closely logged, and punishments paid out without regard to rank or station. Crew either learned from their mistakes or transferred to other ships. The survivors of her wrath thereafter maintained a very high rate of excellence and included a number of seriously over-qualified crew members who had later gone on to other posts and shined.

Jessica counted the names as they were read off. It was an all-hands meeting, so there were twenty-one pilots and flight crew present, plus one senior engineer. They sounded generally bored, perhaps a touch sullen, as if meetings were beneath them.

Based on the pilots she had known, any time not out-ship flying was generally time that was wasted. Opportunities lost. Years of chasing pirates down and rarely catching them would wear.

That was going to change, too.

Jessica perked up as Iskra's voice changed timber. It was never soft, but it gained something, like what you would use to drive nails through boards.

"Okay," the woman said. "You're all here, you've heard the news, the rumors, and the gossip. We'll leave Jumpspace at *Simeon* in twenty-six hours."

That was greeted with groans and hoots. About normal for people who considered themselves hotshot pilots.

"Iskra," a man's voice cut through the noise. "Don't you have anything better for us? I've flown the range at *Simeon* seven times now. It's getting predictable."

The voice sounded like it belonged to a young man who was used to giving orders. The tone was a good, rich, penetrating baritone. It probably went over well with the ladies at ports of call and dockside bars. Reviewing the roster in her head, Jessica was pretty sure who the owner was, as well.

"Well, *Jouster*," the Flight Deck Commander replied, hard, heavy, "I'd like to be the one to ruin your day, but I got outvoted. Ladies and gentlemen, I will now turn the floor over the Command Centurion Keller for your briefing."

Jessica stepped in from the side hall and surveyed the group as she walked to the lectern. They scrambled to their feet in surprise as their commander walked in.

Iskra was a little taller but very blond. The assembled crew represented about every ethnicity in the Republic, bound together by service and experience. Most of them scowled at her. She returned the favor.

Darya Lagunov was in the third row, next to a short, dark, curvy woman who was at pains to ignore the tall, blond viking of a giant on her other side. Similar dynamics played out around her. They had obviously been together long enough to develop cliques, but not long enough for feuds.

Jessica let her scowl embrace them all for a few seconds, and then smiled. That seemed to unsettle them even more.

She found *Jouster*, Senior Flight Centurion Milos Pavlovic, the Flight Commander, seated off-center in the second row, about three meters away. He certainly looked the part of a hot-shot pilot and erstwhile ladies' man.

Brown hair, blue eyes, lantern jaw. Exuded a raw sexuality. Noble-born from one of the bluest of the blue-blood clans. A man born with a silver spoon in his mouth and all the advantages money and connections could bring.

Jessica was willing to give him the benefit of the doubt just from his service record. He should have gone into command, and would probably have been serving as executive officer on a cruiser now Instead, he liked to fly, and was really good at it.

He was just now coming to his feet, well after everyone else. Jessica let her smile settle on him. That chip on the shoulder was the reason he was stationed clear the hell out here, instead of on the main frontier. That, and a history with the daughters of Fleet Lords.

It was a shame that First Lord Kasum had been unwilling to provide her a better Flight Commander. Or, as he had explained it, "There isn't a better flyer out there. And I don't have time for you to break a new leader in."

"Be seated," Jessica said quietly into the silence. She waited for them to settle and the coughing and rustling to stop.

"To make *Simeon* interesting for you," she purred, "you'll land short, run the range on guns alone, engage every target, and you won't be done until there are kill-hits on everything in scan range."

Jessica waited for the sudden surge of noise to die down. She watched *Bitter Kitten* turn to her compatriot with an evil, victorious smile. She imagined bets were going to be settled after this.

The young man in front raised his hand to get her attention.

"Yes, *Jouster?*" she inquired.

"Just how short were you planning to execute the jump, commander?" He managed to combine bored, sarky, and superior all in one tone.

Truly, a marvel of a man. However could she resist the raw charisma of his money and breeding? Gosh, princess. Watch.

"We'll come out of Jumpspace a light hour out after our second exit, get our bearings, and jump again, *Jouster,*" she replied, mimicking his tone almost perfectly. Others in the room noticed before he did. "The entire wing will execute a crash-launch when we come out at the entry to the range and go about your business."

"Crash launches are dangerous, commander," he scowled as he spoke, glancing about for support from his mates. The room seemed poised with anticipation. Of what, she wasn't sure, but she certainly had their undivided attention.

Jessica refrained from smiling. She would probably look like a cat if she did right now.

"War is dangerous business, Centurion," she replied with a verbal whip-crack. "I'd rather you made your amateur mistakes on a safe range than when it counted. Any other questions?"

One of the older pilots raised his hand. Holly Dyson had a shaved head, lanky build, and a handlebar mustache. And a reputation in the fleet for crazy stunts. Crazy by the extreme standards of pilots. Another one exiled when he should be in the thick of things.

"Go ahead, *Gaucho*," she said.

"Did you mean the *whole* wing would crash launch, sir? Everybody?" he asked. He had a pleasant tenor voice with an odd accent.

"Assault shuttles also have guns on them. The wing will be graded on time, not efficiency."

That triggered another round of murmurs rippling around the room.

Bitter Kitten spoke up from the back. "Why guns only, commander?"

Jessica smiled warmly back at her. *Bitter Kitten* knew some of what was coming, but had obviously kept a few tidbits to herself. That was useful to know.

"Because I intend to operate well at sea for extended periods. That means we don't get to run home for more missiles if we shoot them all off at the first fleeing pirate we encounter. I want to know that you can kill things at knife-fighting ranges if we have to. It's going to be dangerous out there."

She let the smile fade and surveyed the room with a hard eye. "Any other questions?"

The silence hung. It was not the stillness of acquiescence. More likely shock. It would wear off. Or not.

"Then I will leave you with Senior Centurion Vlahovic for the rest of your briefing."

She marched back to the open side door and exited. Once outside, she closed the door and smiled at Marcelle, who had listening silently outside.

"So what do you think, Marcelle?" she asked quietly.

"Lambs to the slaughter, boss."

"Us or them?"

Marcelle smiled broadly. "I don't know anybody who's dumb enough to bet against you."

Jessica let a breath out to try to relax. Command meant being right, being decisive, and being indestructible. It was only going to get harder from here.

CHAPTER XIII

Date of the Republic October 6, 392 Jumpspace approaching Simeon

Jessica walked onto the bridge and surveyed the scene. The tension fairly cracked.

That was good. She wanted them at a higher pitch than normal for what she had planned.

In one hand, another stack of hand-written linen envelopes. Being able to write those ahead of time required one to plan for a number of contingencies.

It was just one of the things she had learned from the man who would go on to be First Lord. How to fight wars.

Amateurs studied tactics. Professionals studied strategy. Conquerors studied logistics.

Tamara Strnad was already settled into the Central Station. She turned a questioning eye on Jessica, but Jessica shook her head. Up until now, it had been a test to see how well the crew could handle suddenly having to take charge.

They had done rather well. That was the test of Jež as the man who had been responsible for training them and keeping them on task. She had expected him to pass.

Now it was going to get messy. This was where the fun would start.

Or the failure.

Jessica walked next to Tamara and gave her a warm smile. She leaned in close as she handed the woman the next stack of envelopes and whispered, "Final exam, Centurion. Good luck."

Tamara nodded back at her and looked down at the stack. The top one had the words *Open three minutes before you exit Jumpspace* scrawled neatly on the outside in Jessica's careful hand.

Jessica moved to a training station off to one side of the long, skinny bridge, opposite from the one Jež had commandeered, and examined the crew. Today just might make or break them.

"Astrogation systems," Tamara called out, "please put a countdown timer on the main screen for emergence from Jumpspace."

"Roger that, sir," Zupan called back, her hands dancing across the virtual keyboard in a fantastically-complex piano sonata. Numbers appeared on the screen, slowly ticking down.

"Flight Deck," Tamara continued. Jessica could detect a hint of stress in the words, but she was handling it well, especially given the curveballs she was being thrown. "Five minutes to first hop. Wake up your pilots and make sure they're ready. I expect second hop to end in fifty-five minutes."

Jessica watched a message begin to scroll across the bottom of the main viewscreen. *Flight Deck green and green. Two crews ready for emergency launch at first emergence. Iskra*

Jessica nodded. Exactly by the book. It was a shame the book wasn't going to be worth much in a few days. If she was lucky.

She watched Tamara open the first envelope and read the contents. Her black hair was just long enough to move as she looked down. It bobbed as she re-read the entire letter and then glanced up at Jessica with one arched eyebrow that melted into an evil grin after a moment.

Jessica nearly giggled with delight. This wasn't *Brightoak's* crew, but they were damned good.

"Flag Centurion Zivkovic," Tamara called with a strong lilt to her voice, "We will expect to rendezvous with our squadron on emergence. Prepare squadron channels and make sure Flag facilities are ready."

Jessica heard a squeak, from the young man seated next to her. Encj Zivkovic was a brilliant man from a poor family, so they had a few things in common, but he lacked the killer instinct that would have marked him for eventual command.

Jessica wondered if she could help him find it.

She watched him recover his poise with a quick glance at her, and then begin toggling switches live that had been dark on his station.

The next words surprised Jessica.

"Defense Systems," she heard Tamara call, "prepare to bring all defensive shields and weapon systems on line to engage possible hostiles. Gunnery, there should be two vessels when we arrive, the heavy destroyer *Rajput*, and a fleet escort, *CR-264*. I want you to unlock everything and plot generic firing solutions. You will refine those as soon as we have any signals. If this is a trap, I want you to kill the biggest target you have first, but you will not fire without a direct order."

Jessica smiled. It was the kind of order she had given a number of times, even approaching the fleet's home base at *Ladaux*.

"Primaries as well, ma'am?" a young man asked nervously from in front of her.

"Affirmative," Tamara replied calmly. "Primaries, Secondaries, missiles, and kitchen sinks."

"Acknowledged." The two weapons officers managed to speak in perfect synch.

"I will need authorization to unlock the weapon systems, sir," the older one, the man in charge of gunnery, continued.

"Stand by," Tamara replied as she flipped through the envelopes in front of her.

Jessica had already left her seat and approached quickly. "It's not there, Strnad," she said quietly. "Allow me?"

Tamara looked up with a smile. "Thanks, commander."

Jessica concentrated as she typed. The code was a random ten-digit hash of numbers and letters. "It's against regulations to have it written down anywhere other than in the safe. Even for training exercises, but you would have been able to retrieve it from there, if I was really dead."

"Aye, sir." She looked relieved.

Jessica returned to her seat and buckled the belt, just in case.

She watched her Tactical Officer, nee-Commander, take a deep breath. "Emergence in thirty seconds."

Enej Zivkovic looked at the once-unfamiliar Flag console layout and memorized the current settings and placements. Normally, he handled piloting and sensor duties, but he had spent the last few days in a crash course.

There was nothing about being a Flag Centurion he couldn't handle.

Coordinate communications with the rest of the squadron for a Fleet Lord, or, in this case, a senior Command Centurion in charge. Make the occasional tactical observation for the commander, translate broad tactical commands into specific orders for ships on the fly.

Make sure everybody was on task.

It was basically multi-level chess, in real time. He was good at that. Why the new commander had put him in charge wasn't something he was going to ask. It was a gift horse kind of thing. And momma always told him not to look gift horses in the mouth.

Besides, he was used to being much smarter than his commanders. Enej wasn't so sure with this one. Something about the way she moved and looked at people.

And those envelopes were really cool. Totally archaic, and yet perfect for conducting this kind of field exercise. There was no way someone could hack the computer file and read things ahead of time. Not that he would ever try.

"Emergence in thirty seconds," Second Officer Strnad intoned across the silent bridge.

Enej called up the stats for *Rajput* and *CR-264* and slid them to one side of his screen.

Rajput was an older design, even older than he was.

Let's see, class ship and the only one ever built.

Dramatically up-gunned standard destroyer design, all guns and no butter, as his father would have said. Almost tough enough to take on a light cruiser, but too fragile, plus cramped and extremely hard to maintain. *Useful if you needed to kick a door in, not so good in a general fleet engagement.*

He could see why she ended up out here, the only one of her kind.

CR-264 was more interesting, anyway. After eighteen years as a *Type: Cutter/Revenue*, she had impressed into the Republic Navy as a very light corvette, and classed as a Fleet Escort. The rest of the class had been eventually retired, and they didn't even make them anymore. Cutters these days were smaller and operated in packs. And Corvettes were larger.

Enej checked the readout again to be sure. *CR-264's* whole weapons system consisted of two Type-2 beams forward and four Type-3 beams, two on each side? *That's it?* Hell, *Auberon's* two S-11 Saturation fighters and her Gunship were more heavily armed. But she could also go nearly a year without resupply if her environmental systems were well-tuned and the crew was careful about what they grew and what they ate?

Really? A whole year?

He made a note to look up the history of the class when he got off duty. That didn't sound right, but it was kinda awesome if it was.

Nobody did that any more.

"Ten seconds to emergence," came the call. Enej turned his attention back to the console.

One quick pass confirmed that everything was ready. *Auberon* was broadcasting her ID signal, scrambled on the latest fleet cypher. Daniel Giroux had the Sciences systems on full passive scan. Tobias Brewster was ready to shoot anything that moved. Nina Vanek had the defensive screens on and all the Type-1 and Type-2 defensive beams charged.

And…blink.

Some people couldn't feel a ship come out of Jumpspace. Enej always thought that was weird, because it would wake him from a dead sleep. It wasn't bad, just a hiccup, or maybe a ripple across the community swimming pool. But there it was.

His board came live quickly.

Okay. Rajput is there, closer in to the entrance of the weapons range. CR-264 was keeping station, escorting her against anybody coming out to play. We landed a little short. No, scratch that. We landed perfectly for them to go from a dead stop to come up to speed with us so they could blink hop briefly into Jumpspace and come out over there to run the range. That was pretty good timing.

"Commander," he said, training putting his brain on autopilot, "We have identified *Rajput* and *CR-264*. Squadron and Flag communications are on channel four in standard cypher."

Time to earn his keep.

Tamara practiced her Command Scowl. What was about to happen might be the most fun she had on this entire cruise, but commanders weren't supposed to smile.

Command was serious business.

Zivkovic seemed to be handling the Flag Centurion duties well. Everyone else was on pins and needles. And only she knew what Commander Keller had planned.

She pushed the button that projected her voice everywhere, including inside the refrigerator on E-deck and the aft female toilets on B. "*Auberon*, this is the bridge," she intoned. "We have made it to *Simeon* and met up with the rest of our squadron. We will shortly return to Jumpspace and then make a short hop. All hands to battle stations."

Lights went red everywhere.

Tamara had always wanted to do that. *That* was what command was all about. She suppressed a giggle.

"Flag Centurion," she continued, trying to be calm and knowing her voice was too bright, "I am transmitting a sailing plan to your station. Communicate it to the entire squadron immediately and have them prepare for jump."

She watched Enej push his buttons and talk into a sound-deadening microphone.

Tamara knew the message had been conveyed when the Pilot actually turned and looked at her across the bridge. Nada Zupan, the Pilot, didn't say anything, but the look conveyed a wealth of surprise and confusion, followed the same sort of evil grin Tamara was fighting to keep off her face right now.

They both glanced at the Gunnery Centurion, Tobias Brewster. *The Creator's gift to the women of the fleet. Just ask him. The favored son of a major Fleet Lord, scion of the family. Etcetera, etcetera, etcetera.*

Tamara was pretty sure every female on the ship had a *Tobias* story to tell, as well as several of the men.

The best revenge, bucko, is served ice cold.

Tamara counted down the moments for the second hop to complete.

She knew she was keyed up, but what was about to happen was something *Auberon* had never done before, as far as she knew with this crew.

The tactical plot went live as they dropped into real space. No more estimates. Hard scan figures began to fill in the spaces around them.

"Flag, have the Flight Deck crash launch the entire wing now," she said, trying to bounce calmness off the bulkheads when she really wanted to hoot and dance.

"Orders are as before with one change. We will rendezvous with the entire wing at point *Epsilon*." Tamara waited for that to register on people's minds. *Who was paying attention besides Keller?*

On her workstation's screen, she saw the three big blips line up, just like she had ordered. Exactly wrong from the standard Order of Battle. *CR-264* was in the lead, rather than tucked in close on a flank. *Rajput* was lined up with the other two and at the tail of the line, but on a higher elevation where she could bring her guns to bear across the entire engagement sphere.

Tamara reached down and toggled a physical switch. It was one of the few on her console that was not a video touchscreen. It had a nice, reassuring solidity as it clicked into place.

For a moment, victory leaked out all over her face. She quickly squelched it.

"*Auberon*, this is the bridge," she calmly announced. "All weapons are set to training mode until further notice. Flag, have the squadron conform to our maneuvers. Helm, come to heading 351 by 10 by 18 and accelerate to flank speed. We will be running down Lane 4 to engage a hostile battle squadron. Initiate training exercise."

Tamara leaned back and sucked in a deep breath silently.

On her left, she watched slow horror dawn on the face of the Gunnery officer. He had apparently only now caught up with her. On her right, Tamara watched the defensive systems, shields, short-range missiles, and smaller beam emplacements come live and cycle through their targeting solutions.

Downrange, satellites and automated combat simulators came live as *Auberon* approached.

Tamara almost felt out of body as she watched. Normally, the duty of the Second Officer was to oversee tactical duties. The Commander issued priorities, she picked targets, and Nina Vanek would engage them with all the full defensive array.

Tobias Brewster, the Gunnery Centurion, almost never had anything to do.

Hell, Tamara couldn't even remember the last time the Secondaries had been fired in anger, let alone the monstrous Primaries.

Maybe, if he hadn't been such an asshole, she would have given him more than a few seconds warning.

Tamara looked over again at the perfect hair and perfectly-manicured nails, and remembered the last time he had propositioned her.

Then again, maybe not.

Jessica watched the by-play around her as *Auberon* came out of Jumpspace and aligned for combat. Without Jež in charge, some interesting dynamics came to the fore, as she had expected they would.

The Gunnery Centurion was the most entertaining.

Jessica had watched every other person on the bridge running through some sort of simulation, usually as a training refresher, or at least to fill the time, while they had made both jumps. Brewster had apparently spent his time thinking deep thoughts.

Certainly, he hadn't been preparing.

Right now, he was scrambling to align the weapon turrets, something he should have done the moment they came back into space.

Jessica wrote herself a quick note on a clipboarded piece of paper. Written records lasted forever, but weren't in any system unless she chose to add them. It was a useful filing system.

Because they made very little sound themselves, each weapon was coded to a tone so the bridge crew could identify them. The defensive array, a Type-2 and two Type-1's on each flank, pulsed in a staccato symphony as they fired. *The Music of War*, some wag had called it, once upon a time.

On her screen, Jessica watched as the flight wing emerged like angry hornets and set off down Lane 6 to test their mettle strafing and dogfighting, escorted into battle by the Gunship *Necromancer* and leading the Assault Shuttle *Cayenne* behind.

What idiot painted a dropship bright red, anyway?

A deeper, pulsed tone, got her attention. *Auberon* had fired one of her two Primaries at a closing automaton meant to simulate a destroyer. And missed. Badly. She ticked a mark on her page.

Tamara responded by pushing *Auberon* down hard into a new plane, like a submersible vessel going for deep water. Ahead, *CR-264* turned enough to fire everything she had at the drone, not that it would do much, but in battle, it might distract a crew. *Rajput* came over the top like the cavalry and fired everything she had into the target in one narrow salvo of ravening destructive fury.

Orders flew thick and fast about her as she listened. *CR-264* was about to be surrounded by a wolfpack of simulated corvettes and mauled, badly out of position as a result of saving *Auberon*.

This time, *Auberon's* other Primary hit, taking one of the enemy vessels off-line.

The Type-3's lanced out as well, scoring a hit and distracting the enemy ships as *CR-264* blasted straight through the gap and *Rajput* cycled her weapons into the fray.

A sepulchral tune indicated that Auberon had sustained a hit in the exchange.

Apparently, a missile had gotten through and was rated as a hit by the gaming computer. Jessica checked the simulated destruction and listened to the Damage Control Parties wade into the fray on the lower decks.

It had been a long time since she had seen combat scores so low. Jessica made more notes. She really missed *Brightoak*.

CHAPTER XIV

Jessica sat at her desk, in her new office, and scowled her most fierce scowl. Often, it was for show. Today, she was truly angry.

Career-destroying angry.

"And when I reviewed the statistics for the exercise," she continued, cold, sharp, deathly as she looked at the man's face, "I note that you scored a forty-seven percent hit ratio. That is the worst I have ever seen in the field. Fortunately, for you, it is not the worst score ever recorded for *Simeon*, so your name doesn't go up on the wall over there."

She paused, letting the energy bleed off instead of building to a peak.

Across from her, sitting perfectly still and as white as a ghost, Gunnery Centurion Tobias Brewster looked like he was trying to disappear from sight.

She let the moment drag. Brewster did not appear to be a popular person, either with his comrades or his subordinates. Unlike, say, the Engineer, Ozolinsh, or her new Flag Centurion. There was nothing in Brewster's records, but the rumors had been there. Wealth, power, upbringing. A bully and a Don Juan. And a disciple of the former commander, Kwok, who was a scion of Loncar.

Jessica looked through the young man.

To his credit, he sat perfectly still and met her gaze.

"Do you have anything to say for yourself, mister?" she rasped, anger threatening to overflow.

"It's not my fault," he offered weakly, failing in his attempt to sound charming.

"It most assuredly is, Brewster," she pounced, fingers tapping the desk ominously. "Your weapons. Your station. Your failure."

She watched him blink. He swallowed past a throat that sounded tight.

"I can do better," he finally said.

Jessica's chin came up. "Can you?" she said. "Can you really? Because I would be happy to sign your transfer request right now. You could be off this ship in a few hours and back to a cushy job in days."

"No, ma'am," he said. She could see him getting his feet under him as he spoke. "I screwed up, but I can salvage it."

"Not on my bridge, Brewster," she growled, "but I will make you a deal, if you are interested."

"Sir?"

"I will disrate you as a Gunner, right now, and transfer you down to the emergency bridge," she continued. "You can requalify from scratch on every weapons system, on every simulation lane at *Simeon*. Or you can transfer out right now and I will put nothing at all in your record to indicate that we ever had this conversation. What will it be?"

"Everyone will know, sir," he said, morose.

"That's not my problem, Brewster. I'm not the one who was completely unprepared and tried to set a record low score."

"I'm better that that, commander," he pleaded. "I can prove it to you."

Jessica considered the young man before her. A single day had aged him several years. At this rate, he might be a grown-up soon.

"If you stay," she said finally, "I will work you like a dog. Every scut duty will be yours until someone else screws up worse. And the offer to let you go free will be off the table. The only way out after you leave this room will be to resign your commission."

She fixed him with a hard stare.

He flinched for a moment, and then met her squarely.

"What will it be, Brewster?" she asked.

"I'll stay, sir," he said quietly.

She nodded. "Report to the Emergency Bridge for your next shift, then. And may the Creator have mercy on your soul."

Tobias Brewster stood and saluted her. Technically incorrect indoors, but he did it well, and it seemed to come from the heart.

There might be something salvageable from this punk after all.

She nodded to his salute. "Send Vanek in when you go."

"Aye, sir." And he was gone.

Jessica took a deep breath and tried to control her anger at Brewster. Even in defeat, he was trying to charm his way out of being sent to the principal's office.

It probably worked to his benefit most of the time.

The door opened and the Defense Centurion stepped in.

Jessica sized her up.

Nina Vanek was a small woman. No, petite. Almost a waif. Jessica had felt like a giant standing next to her, or an ogre. According to the personnel files, Vanek had nearly washed out of the Academy on more than one occasion for being underweight, in spite of the best work of three physical fitness instructors and a dietician.

She entered now with a stack of books, actual paper volumes from the ship's library from the look of them, and a portable projector under one arm.

"Ma'am," Nina said simply and came to as close to attention as she could without spilling everything.

"Sit, Centurion," Jessica said. "Explain all this, please."

She watched the tiny woman set the books to one side and the projector in the middle of her desk.

She did not turn it on, yet.

Nina took the seat and visibly marshalled her thoughts. Then she stopped and re-thought them, again, apparently. "I scored eighty-seven percent on the run at *Simeon*," she said. "Passable, but we would still be in drydock for several months after suffering at least two major hits."

"Correct, Vanek," Jessica interjected in the gap. "It takes one hit to wound you, and generally three to kill. Two is iffy, depending on the location, but I agree with your assessment."

"Aye, sir," Vanek replied. "The Strike Carrier, our lady *Auberon*, seems to have a design flaw. They exploited it at *Simeon*. All's fair in love and war, but I'm not sure how we can survive if the Imperials do the same thing."

Jessica felt herself dropping back into Tactical Instructor Mode. She could hear Kasum's voice coming out of her mouth. It felt weird.

"Describe the scenario, Nina," she said.

"Yes, ma'am," the tiny woman reached out and powered on the projector. *Auberon* and her escorts appeared in blue. The enemy drones were green. It played a high speed loop that ended with several simulated explosions along *Auberon's* right flank.

"According to the standard tactics manuals," Nina continued, "we were subject to what they call a Saturation Overload. They can put more missiles in the air than we can kill, unless we hold back part of the flight wing, and keep at least one escort in close. It's why Fleet Carriers normally have so many escorts around them. Strike Carriers are even more vulnerable."

"And that's why they so rarely go into direct combat," Jessica agreed. "How would you prepare for it?"

Nina's face screwed up in concentration. "If we were expecting it, we could cycle the missile launchers down and keep a shot missile in the primary slot. One of those will disrupt either a wing of fighters, or, like we got hammered with at the range, a flight of missiles."

"Correct," Jessica replied, "what's the downside?"

"We functionally lose one or both of the missile launchers by shifting into defensive mode. Cuts down on our killing power right at the time we need it most."

"Exactly, Centurion," Jessica felt her mood soften. "That's why they do that. This is generally a no-win scenario for a Tactical team. It's one of the things Lane 4 is designed to teach you."

"Aye, ma'am," Nina replied quietly. "But Burley had an interesting solution." She touched one of the books in front of her.

Jessica blinked in surprise. There might be a way to beat a Saturation Overload?

Jessica noted a piece of paper marking a page. Nina Vanek flipped the book open and shoved the table across to her.

Jessica considered the words of a tactical prophet dead nearly five hundred years.

Interesting.

"So, Vanek," she asked as she finished, "how would you suggest we implement it? Burley's idea of putting a spare missile launcher in to replace one of our shuttle bays won't work unless we lose the ability to crash-launch the flight wing easily."

"Yes, ma'am. But what if we did this?"

Vanek toggled the projector to bring up a schematic of *Auberon*, slowly rotating along her long axis. A blister along her spine turned red and transformed into something else as they watched.

"This is the secondary observation tower, commander," Nina said quietly. "I checked the logs and the last time it was officially used was eight years ago. And then only to verify that it still worked after the last major overhaul in drydock. The need for such a tool dates back thousands of years, to a time when artificial life-forms controlled most spaceships. If your ship's personality died, you had to calculate everything manually, using a real, honest-to-Creator, glass telescope, a mass spectrometer, and a stellar encyclopedia."

Jessica leaned forward and touched the projection. It stopped and swelled out.

"Go on," she said, intrigued. She had never heard of someone taking Burley this direction.

"So if we remove the telescope from the armature and insulate the room, sir, we could weld a missile rack on instead. Wire it up to the defensive array, and we could pop it open when we went into combat. Put a pair of shot missiles on them, and we've got a really nasty ace in the hole next time someone tries that trick on us."

Jessica leaned back and considered. There was nothing in the regulations about removing the secondary observatory. As Nina said, it was a tradition dating back to computer automation, before navigators had to memorize routes and stars in order to do their jobs. *The Dark Ages of The Immortals.* The Artificially Intelligent Lifeforms. Before mankind had outgrown them.

She considered the design and layout of the new weapons system.

"How long have you been working on this design, Centurion?" Jessica asked.

"It came to me this morning in the shower, ma'am," Nina replied, apparently trying to shrink in on herself.

"This morning?" she said, surprise evident in her voice.

"Yes, ma'am."

"Have Ozolinsh dedicate one of his engineers to the design," Jessica said. "We'll have a meeting with the engineering staff in three days and see what it would take to make it work. One thing, though. Everything has to be able to be replaced at the end of the tour. Dismissed."

"Aye, sir," Nina smiled and rose. She gathered all of her materials under her arms and practically skipped out of the room.

Jessica smiled. At least something good was going to come of this day. She hoped.

CHAPTER XV

Date of the Republic October 10, 392 Jumpspace outbound from Simeon system

The room normally served many purposes, including training classes and design labs. Today, all the of the workstations were turned flat. Only the big screen at the far end was active.

Jessica looked down the long conference table in the Engineering design bay at the people who shared her space.

Engineers sat along both sides of the table, coming in every shape and flavor, down to Nina Vanek and one of Ozolinsh's engineers standing in front of a projection that slowly rotated.

The woman standing with Vanek might be the only person in the entire crew Nina's size. She wore a Yeoman's uniform that came in the smallest size available and was still baggy on her. Jessica thought the woman might be half a head shorter than her own short height. And she fairly radiated pixie, with a slim, petite build, and a smile that could warm up a room.

"Any questions?" the black-haired beauty asked. She spoke with a strange accent, almost barbaric in its slurring of consonants and stretching vowels out. Jessica presumed, without looking, that she might have been born in the borders beyond the edges of the *Republic* and the *Fribourg Empire*, and had only emigrated closer to the galactic core as a teenager.

Jessica watched as every head at the table slowly turned to face her, including the Chief Engineer. The conference room was pregnant with anticipation. Stories of what she had already done to the few crew members who failed to measure up had gotten around.

"I'm interested, Vanek," she drawled, "as to why you plan to remove the bay doors completely and then cover the bay back over."

She watched Nina smile at her and nod to her cohort.

"I'll let Moirrey explain," Vanek replied

"Is quite simple, ma'am," the pixie began. Moirrey Kermode had a voice like a songbird, a very small one, her tone floating up and down and around as she spoke. "You won't want anyone in there when we launch birds, anyway. Doing it this way saves you four to six seconds in an emergency. Take the doors off, and cover the whole thing over with a cloth that will hold until we push a missile through it. It won't show on scanners and the bad guys won't be able to tell the difference until we fly one. Then it won't matter. After all, all the world's a stage."

"A stage?" Jessica was at a loss.

"Aye, ma'am. An' we are merely players."

"That sounds like a quote, Yeoman Kermode," Jessica observed.

"Tis," the tiny woman smiled. "Shakespeare. The Great Bard."

"I see," Jessica leaned back. Around the table, the rest relaxed as well. "Republic? Empire? Concord?"

"No, ma'am," Moirrey continued. "Homeworld. He lived before spaceships."

"And people still quote him eleven thousand years later?" Jessica asked, startled by the non-sequitur.

"He were a great playwright," she smiled. She raised her hands to encompass the entire ship around them in a single motion. "This is just a set. It needs decorating so people will believe what they see, instead of what they know. Ye show them an observation blip, and they'll belief it until ye shows 'em different."

Jessica smiled as she listened to the woman nearly drift into a cant so obscure as to be impenetrable. She rose and stretched.

"Ozolinsh," she said firmly. "You have my authorization. Let Jež know what you need and give me a rough estimate as to when we can test fire it."

She took a step and a paused, before turning back. "Ladies, good job. I'm not sure what reward will be most appropriate, but we'll talk. I expect that we'll need this surprise before we're done."

She exited amidst general noise and hubbub.

Considering where she planned to go, they were most certainly going to need it at some point.

CHAPTER XVI

Date of the Republic October 23, 392 Surat Thani system

Denis entered the forward gymnasium with trepidation. This was Keller's normal training period, and he knew she preferred solitude. And it wasn't like this couldn't have waited until later.

But it was also a good time to chat with her, without the confines of an office, or rank. Plus, he had heard about it, but never actual seen a live demonstration.

This was too good to pass up.

She was standing in the middle of a cleared area about six meters on a side, wearing a skin-tight body suit that left little of her hard body to the imagination. She was concentrating on the man-shaped training robot in front of her, so he could take the time to appreciate form and movement.

Denis liked women that were taller and thinner. Perhaps more like Marcelle Travere, the commander's personal steward. The rest of his commander was equally hard. Feminine, in her own way, but the femininity of the Amazon warrior, and not the fairy princess. Keller had powerful thighs and shoulders, muscular curves that looked like they would turn to fleshiness and eventually fat if she let herself go.

He couldn't imagine her letting herself go. Ever.

She wore a headband today. Normally, her hair was short enough to be out of the way, so it was probably for sweat rather than vision, although it did keep her hair up and back.

Based on her fighting stance, she was left-handed, but he knew that already. In her left hand, she held a long, straight, single-edged sword, what the combatants called a saber. Instead of something more exotic, it was apparently made of simple steel. Denis wondered what it would be like made from hull metal.

In her right hand, a much shorter blade, heavier, and with a pronounced cross-guard instead of the basket protecting her left hand. From his research, they called it the *main-gauche*, literally, the *left hand*, although it wasn't.

She had turned to a spot where she could see him, even as the fighting robot maneuvered with her.

"Jež," she called. "Important?"

"Negative, ma'am," he called back.

She nodded and continued to move.

The robot mirrored her to some extent, with a long and short blade in each human-like hand, although it fought in the more traditional, right-handed, style.

The machine's long blade flashed out, and Denis got a chance to watch the *Valse d'Glaive*.

Instead of standing still and blocking the blow, as normal fencers would, she dropped to a crouch, with the short blade up to redirect the slash over her head.

At the same time, she thrust forward belt-high with her own saber and swung her foot at her opponent's ankle joint.

Denis decided he would have been simultaneously skewered and tripped on his ass.

The robot skipped backwards instead, flashing out with its short blade at her arm.

Rather than try to block, she tumbled across the floor like an acrobat. In the middle of her somersault, Denis heard the loud thump of steel on plastic. The robot stopped suddenly and came to rest.

"Contact: Keller. Score 10 to 5. Match: Keller," a woman's voice announced.

Denis watched Jessica stand and bow ceremonially to the fighting robot.

She turned and walked over to a weapons rack set by the door to the shower and began to inspect her blades.

Denis waited a few moments and then joined her. Only when he got close could he tell how hard she was breathing.

"Jež," she glanced up at him.

"Commander," he nodded back.

"What can I do for you?" she asked.

"We will have gotten the last load of food and supplies within the next twenty minutes and be ready to break orbit. Then we can go do whatever it is we're going to do." He fought the urge to come to parade rest. "It would be useful to know what we're doing."

"And I haven't been particularly forthcoming, have I?" she smiled.

The blades were put away. She grabbed a handy towel and wiped her face and neck.

Up close, Denis had an even better view of the petite amazon body, and the smell. How someone that covered in sweat could manage to smell like a clear morning after rain, he wasn't sure.

It must have been one of those secrets women only passed down to their daughters.

It was also rather distracting at a time when he was trying to be friendly instead of proper. Especially since she apparently was wearing just enough of a sports bra under the top to keep her breasts contained. Not that they were large or heavy, but her sweat seemed to outline them well.

"Command prerogative," he said, falling back on formal instead of friendly. His eyes wanted to wander.

Something of his discomfort seemed to show. She flipped the towel down over her shoulders and covered enough of her body to break his distraction. She smiled, probably aware of the effect she was having.

She was always three steps ahead.

"And you have anticipated me by about two hours," she said, facing him squarely, "which is the mark of a good officer. I had planned to let people know after we crossed to Jumpspace, to keep any hint of our mission from outrunning us."

"I see, commander," he replied. "I can wait."

"No," she said sharply. She paused for a moment, apparently looking for the words before she continued.

"It's not in my nature to trust, Denis. I'm working on it, but it comes hard to me." She licked her lips as she concentrated.

"We're going to go raid *2218 Svati Prime*, on the Imperial side of the *Cahllepp Frontier*."

Denis did some quick math in his head. "That's nearly three weeks sail from here," he said with surprise. "Clear across the *Kaldwell Gulf.*

"Yes," she replied with a hard grin. "They'll never see it coming. That's why we stopped at *Surat Thani* to take on as many supplies as we could hold. It's like a thumb that sticks out into the Gulf itself along here, and makes it a shorter jump. Commercial ships normally run a horseshoe-shaped trade route clear out beyond the borders and back. We're cutting straight across."

She paused, but he had no more questions.

"So you take us out and get us lined up for the Jump," she said, "while I get cleaned up and join you on the bridge in about three hours. I'll let everyone know then."

"I see," he said. Finally, he did, at least a glimmer.

In addition to trials by fire and combat, they were apparently going to become famous for acts of extreme navigation.

He looked down at the weapons rack beside her once again.

As they say, live by the sword…

CHAPTER XVII

***Date of the Republic October 25, 392 Jumpspace outbound from Surat
Thani system***

Fidgets? Really? Now?

Jessica sat at her desk, reviewed random notes while she waited. And fidgeted

She was generally good at waiting. One former commander had likened her to a moray eel more than once, tucked down into a dark hole and waiting for something interesting to swim overhead.

Today, she just had the fidgets. It was unlike her, but this was an abnormal day.

A knock at the hatch broke her out of her reverie.

"Enter," she called, pushing a button on her desk to unlock it from the inside.

Marcelle came through first, carefully, as though scouting her mood. Apparently, the fidgets had been obvious. Or perhaps contagious. They shared a quick, secret smile before Marcelle gestured for her companion to enter.

Yeoman Kermode, Moirrey, was extremely nervous.

Perhaps a touch guilty? Called suddenly to the headmaster's office because somebody blabbed? All hell about to break loose and the past going to suddenly catch up with you?

Jessica made a mental note not to look too deeply into the woman's past. Perhaps get her drunk sometime and pick her brain, but that could be later.

"Sit, please, Moirrey," Jessica said, pointing at one of the chairs. She looked up with a smile. "Thank you, Marcelle. I promise to be nice to her."

Marcelle actually blushed. "Aye, sir," she said and was gone out the door.

Jessica took a moment to study the young engineer before she said anything.

She was tiny.

Not as ethereal as Nina Vanek, although they were almost of a height. No, it was someone had taken a perfectly-proportioned woman and shrunk her down to a ninety percent copy.

Right now, Moirrey had the fidgets as well. There must be something in the air today.

"Relax," Jessica said suddenly into the silence. "Whatever it is, nobody ratted you out. I want your help on a project."

From the way the woman suddenly collapsed back into the chair, Jessica decided whatever it was she was dreading, it must have been good. All the more reason not to dig. And to take her drinking sometime.

"I was impressed with the solution you came up with for Vanek's missile launcher," Jessica continued. "I would like you to think of this as your reward for a job well done."

"Sir?" the woman asked. The voice was even tinier than the body right now, very much unlike the confident, competent engineer Jessica had seen making the presentation.

"By now," Jessica continued, "everyone knows we are going to raid *2218 Svati Prime*. They don't know why."

Jessica paused to observe. Moirrey was recovering her aplomb, slowly. Good enough.

"We'll have the firepower to destroy their local defenses. It's just a small mining colony, so it's not that important. And, please keep this secret, it is only our first stop. I plan to hit several worlds over there before heading home."

Moirrey nodded at her with a card-sharp look in her eyes. There was a fire brewing inside, if slowly.

"I looked up your playwright," Jessica said. "Even watched one of his plays, translated out of the ancient tongue. He was a master showman, Moirrey."

"Aye, sir," the Yeoman replied. "One of the best the race has e'er birthed."

"It got me to thinking," Jessica continued. "I would like to do something that leaves a lasting psychological scar on the *Fribourg Empire*."

"Are we going to bomb them, sir?" She got a nervous look in her eyes.

Jessica shook her head. "No, Yeoman," she said sharply. "That would just piss them off, and invite retaliations on our worlds. *2218 Svati Prime* isn't worth hardly anything in the grand scheme of things."

"I see." Moirrey said meekly. "Sorry about that, sir."

"No," Jessica said. "It was a good question, Moirrey. I was thinking about how all the world is a stage. I want you to build me something that is all flash. It doesn't need substance. The substance is the fear it will invoke, up and down the Imperial frontier, that they might be next."

Moirrey leaned forward with a tight, wicked smile. Jessica knew, right then, that she had the right person.

"Limitations, sir?" Moirrey asked.

"Keep civilian casualties to an absolute minimum, Kermode," Jessica said. "Preferably zero. Dead enemies are martyrs. Frightened ones have to be protected."

"Aye, sir," she replied, licking her lips, warming to her topic. "It'll be just like designing a stage set. Ye have to induce the belief, but people be willing to play 'long."

"Why did you join the Navy, Moirrey? Seriously?"

The woman lost her pixie look for a moment as her faced turned deadly serious. "There's no money in theater, ma'am."

"I see," Jessica replied simply. "But if I wanted to turn engineering into a special effects department…?"

"Oh, ma'am," Moirrey smiled dreamily. "We'd make the Bard jealous with envy at what we could accomplish, were minds set to mischief."

"Consider yours set to mischief, Yeoman. I'll have a talk with Ozolinsh about your workload going forward."

"Aye, sir," Moirrey said. "I'll make ye proud, ma'am."

"I'm counting on it. Dismissed."

She watched Moirrey practically dance out of the room with glee. She felt like she had just let a fox loose in the hen house, but then, hadn't that been what Kasum had done with her?

She looked down at the desk. The fidgets seemed to have left the room with the young woman from engineering.

Now the serious business could start.

Jessica came up from a groggy sleep as her system chirped a message. She was deep in the middle of her sleep period, so it must be one she had flagged important, but not critical enough to rouse her. As if she slept much anyway.

She touched the bedside screen to bring the message up, noted it was from Moirrey. It was entitled simply *Mischief*.

Inside, she found a wealth of design images and technical specifications. Way more than she wanted to deal with at this time of night.

Jessica replied with an acknowledgement and tried to go back to sleep.

Would it be enough?

CHAPTER XVIII

Date of the Republic November 13, 392 Jumpspace approaching 2218 Svati Prime

The Junior Varsity was in charge up on the bridge right now, because everyone important was here for the briefing.

Unlike last time, the pilots were even paying attention.

Jessica looked out over the collected faces of the flight crews, as well as the flight engineers and several of her bridge officers. She took a moment to look over at *Jouster*, the Flight Commander. Most of the pilots were paying attention.

"According to civilian intelligence covering at least the last three standard years," she said to the group, bouncing her unaugmented voice off the back wall, "*2218 Svati Prime* is protected by an Imperial fighter squadron, made up at the old one-man *A-7 model b* snub fighters. Fine against pirates. Useful to overwhelm a single raider. You should be able to slaughter them, even out-numbered."

Jouster was apparently feeling his oats this morning. "That's if they can even launch on such short notice," he sneered. "This is the back end of beyond. The crews here are going to be second rate."

Jessica fixed him with a hard eye for a second. He was smiling the sort of smile the class clown gets when he thinks he's scored a point and wants the whole room to acknowledge his witty awesomeness. Others started to snicker, and then got a good look at the commander's face.

"I don't think, *Jouster*," she smiled back, "that we should necessarily assume incompetence from the kinds of fighter squadron commanders that end up on the frontiers. Or were you speaking from experience?"

A few snickers seemed to come from the side of the room where the flight engineers were seated. The rest of the room had fallen to an awkward, stunned silence.

Jouster looked as if he had been slapped. Probably not the first woman to have done that to him. Most likely the first who could make him sit there and take it.

Jessica let the moment hang a bit longer, but *Jouster* seemed to be over his need to be heard. At least for now.

"We're going to drop into realspace four light hours out, well below the ecliptic plane, just long enough to observe the layout. Then we'll hop closer. Launch order will be *da Vinci* in the scout, followed by the entire flight wing. Saturation wing after that, and then *Necromancer*, the gunship. Questions?"

She watched the Dropship pilot, Dyson, raise his hand with a hopeful smile. "What about *Cayenne*?"

"Search and Rescue only, *Gaucho*," she replied. "You'll be on the deck and ready to launch, but I'm not planning a planetary assault. This time."

"What about *the bomb*?" a female voice piped up from the engineering cluster.

From the emphasis on the words, Jessica presumed that it was an open secret. And not one she was sure she was using. Not yet.

"You kill the defenders first," she said after a beat. "*Rajput* will come up close enough to savage their station and knock it out of use for six months. Then we'll talk about *the bomb*."

"Why not just kill it?" one of the pilots asked from the front row.

"Because, little miss *Bitter Kitten*," Jessica replied with a feral smile. "A badly damaged station has to be repaired, and that takes time, and money, and people. Plus they have to find a new place to house a squadron while they do that."

She watched them soak that up for a second. She took a deep breath and cast caution to the wind.

"I'm not fighting a military war here, people," she said, a deadly earnest note creeping into her tone. "This is an economic and political one. My tools of diplomacy happen to be you, but make no mistake, this is about costing them a lot of time, energy, and resources. You kill a pilot, they have to train a new one. You cripple a station, they have to fix it. You raid a planet, all the others get nervous."

"But bombing civilians?" another pilot asked. He was a tall, blond, viking-looking fellow, one of *Jouster's* two wingmates.

Jessica thought about the information in his file. Friedhelm Hannes Förstner. Call sign *Uller*. A polite young gentleman serving honorably with his enemies, whose family had made it out of the *Fribourg Empire* one step ahead of being arrested and disappeared for being politically unsavory.

"Surprise, *Uller*, is an event that takes place in the enemy commander's mind," she replied, reducing the conversation to just the two of them. It was a trick Kasum had taught her. "We just may end up dropping a very large bomb on *2218 Svati Prime*, but we won't be hitting any cities with it. We will be doing something far more important."

She paused, watched him gulp slightly, nod at her.

"We will be destroying their peace of mind."

CHAPTER XIX

Imperial Founding: 170/11/14. Imperial Traffic Control. 2218 Svati Prime system

His bags were packed, waiting patiently for him in the broom closet. All he had to do was grab them, bip down to the transit station, and catch the next shuttle down to the surface of *Ao-Shun*, one hour and twenty-seven minutes from now.

Not that he was counting them.

Heaven forbid.

He was a good little Imperial bureaucrat, you know.

Work, work, work.

Tomas sipped his coffee and tried to stay awake. His shift ended in thirty-four minutes and then he had an entire three days off coming up.

Paradise.

Stereihofen, the capital, was in early summer right now. Pretty blond girls in barely-there swimwear, lounging on a beach. And redheads. And brunettes. And every flavor in between.

Tomas finished his coffee and stared at the bottom of the mug. More? Or maybe just catnap on the shuttle flight down?

Decisions, decisions.

His control board beeped once. It was the high tone, indicating that someone had just dropped out of Jumpspace and been picked up by the Traffic Control scanners.

Odd. He wasn't expecting any more freighters today. The incoming arrival boards were clear for the next nineteen hours. Probably a yacht on an unscheduled run.

Maybe some pretty little debutante come out to enjoy the beach, and maybe several of her friends. *Ao-shun* wasn't so small as to be insular, but the whole planet had a population of only about five million, heavily tilted towards men.

Tomas sighed. It was a downside of Imperial life that women weren't considered strong enough, tough enough, to handle the kinds of heavy manual labor you got on a mining colony.

It would be nice to live someplace where the gender ratio wasn't three to one against. Even a safe career as an Imperial bureaucrat wasn't automatically enough to pick up girls.

He sighed again. The board plotted his new arrival deep back in the sensor shadow of *Aeocan*, the larger moon. Right at the edge of the safe range for Jumpspace.

He didn't have a direct line of sight to it from here either, so the signal was just a vague blob while he waited for the computers to challenge it and register the ship's identity beacon. If he was lucky, they would spend at least half an hour over there getting their act together, finding their ass, and he could turn them over to Evgeny.

A second beep, lower, made him curse under his breath. The ship was already moving, accelerating even, according to the scanners, so her crew was really on the ball. They would be in direct laser communication range in a few minutes, way too soon for him to ignore them and get an early start on his vacation.

Three rapid beeps, an ascending trill, made him drop his coffee mug.

It bounced off the board, flipped once perfectly in the air, and shattered on the floor. If there had had been anything in it, that would be all over his leg right now.

Over the horizon, back in the shadow of the moon, that one little lost freighter had suddenly turned into three signals. As Tomas watched the board, a dozen more appeared.

He hung with one hand over the emergency alert signal. If he opened the locked-down lid and pushed the button inside, all hell would break loose.

It occasionally happened. Two years ago, a pirate corvette had appeared, seized a freighter, and gotten her away before the fighters could catch up.

But that mess of radar signals over there suggested that the vessel was a carrier. He hadn't heard of any pirates getting their hands on a carrier. That would be an absolutely chilling thought, if they did.

Then a new sound intruded. A high-low chirp, that would repeat forever until someone turned it off. The traffic computers had finally identified the ship's identity beacon.

RAN Auberon.

Oh, shit. An Aquitaine fleet raid? Here?

Tomas crossed himself unconsciously as he flipped the switch open and pushed the button. Red emergency lights came on. The two-note emergency tone was being repeated in every room on the station, and being transmitted down to the surface.

Tomas could imagine people skittering like ants with their hill kicked over.

Aquitaine was here.

CHAPTER XX

It was always like this. Pure. Clean.

In many ways, it was better than sex. Or chocolate.

Jessica felt her brain ascend to a higher plane of consciousness as *Auberon* came out of Jumpspace and leapt into battle.

The big board went from the fuzzy edges of prediction to hard lines as sensors began isolating and identifying everything around them.

Ao-shun below them, a tan and blue marble. *Aeocan* between them and the Imperial Station orbiting geo-synched over Stereihofen. The trailing moon, *Remora*, above and outside them.

"Zupan," Jessica said, waiting for the Pilot to glance over at her. "Dead center. Nicely done, Centurion."

She watched the tall blond elf blush as she went back to playing her symphonies on the navigation board.

Jessica sighed internally. She knew Kwok had never taken the time to recognize the everyday excellence of his crew.

It was amazing what the occasional "Good job," would do for someone's morale.

"Sir," a man's voice came from the opposite side of the bridge, "I have a firing solution."

Jessica turned to look at the gunner who was Tobias Brewster's replacement. Aleksander Afolayan was a junior Centurion who had just barely joined the ship before she did. He was a dark-skinned man with bright blue eyes a ready laugh.

"Confirm, please. *Barn owl* under the pole?" she asked.

"Affirmative, sir," he replied quickly. "From here, we can snap a single stealth missile low, get a gravity slingshot, and most likely catch the station completely blindside."

"Very good, Afolayan," she said. "Hold until the other noise will mask us unleashing that bird. And then fire at will."

"Aye, sir," he smiled.

Jessica thumbed a button to talk to the whole vessel. "Flight Deck, this is the bridge," she intoned. "Crash launch the wing now. Jež, take us up and over the top of the moon. Flag Centurion, squadron to conform to our movement as planned, *CR-264* in the lead, *Rajput* trailing. All guns hot, all enemies hostile."

A chorus of voices filled the air. Iskra sent a scrolling marquee, as always. Jessica leaned back and tried to relax. With any luck, they had such total surprise that this would almost be a training exercise.

They would certainly never catch the Empire so completely asleep again, so they needed to make the most of it.

Below, the entire vessel shivered with the combined bump as *Auberon* began spewing out fighters and a single gunship.

And a single, sneaky missile.

War had just come to the frontier.

CHAPTER XXI

Date of the Republic November 14, 392 2218 Svati Prime

Space was filled with fighters, silently racing downrange.

Jouster took the lead as the wing organized, his team in the lead. The second wing, under Marta Eka, *Southbound*, took up station above and behind his. Farther back and on the flank, the Saturation & Scouting Wing, two big S-11 *Orca* Assault Bombers, and a little P-4 *Outrider* probe fighter. And behind them all, one Kartikeya-class gunship, *Necromancer*, ready to wreak utter havoc.

It was a weird mix of craft. Technically, *Jouster* and his group was outgunned by the twelve old Imperial melee fighters over there, right up to the moment that the S-11's started flinging short-range missiles into the mix.

He couldn't imagine that the Imperials were going to be on the ball enough to get all the pilots scrambled fast enough to matter against his Flight, let alone what they would be facing when the big ships came over the horizon.

"*da Vinci*," *Jouster* called out over the Flight comm, "what's the status over there?"

"Fox in the henhouse, *Jouster*," came the reply. The probe pilot, *da Vinci*, also known as Senior Flight Centurion Ainsley Barret, had probably hacked into their secure channels by now. She did things like that.

Her little craft was completely outclassed by anything the Imperials could throw up, but having her here with a dedicated sensor pod instead of missiles gave him a tactical edge worth half a squadron, all by herself. "Somebody over there hasn't even encrypted. Planetary Governor himself is broadcasting orders in the clear on channel fourteen."

"Roger that. Break. Saturation Wing and *Necromancer*, launch your first wave of missiles now."

Jouster smiled as his sensors picked up the first two Imperials fighters finally launching over there, headed the wrong way and furiously trying to accelerate so they could loop around and engage them. "Might as well see if we can score a hit on the launch bay and put them entirely out of action early."

Jouster looked down at his scanner and tried not to laugh. The Imperials had managed to get six fighters up before a missile had gotten through the defense array and triggered a set of secondary and tertiary explosions, blowing out the module that held the Imperial fighter squadron. Nobody else was coming out to play.

"Team, this is *Jouster*," he called over the comm, "Six on Six, go to melee. *da Vinci*, keep an eye out for anybody coming to help."

A chorus of assents and hoots sounded back at him as his Flight began to close.

"Bombardment wing," he continued, singling out the two S-11's and the gunship. "*Starfall*, *Damocles*, *Necromancer*, prepare for your strafing run on the enemy station. Remember, badly damaged, but not destroyed. Hold fire if you have any doubts."

A bright light appeared over the planet, lighting up the horizon. On his scanner, the side of the Imperial base turned to hash as an explosion blew materials and substance into space.

"All teams, cancel previous orders," he said with a savage joy. "Bombardment wing, the enemy station is down. Repeat, enemy station is down. Go straight at the fighters and get them to run if you can. Fighter Wings, swoop in on them from both sides. Let's dance, people."

"Prisoners?" *Uller* called back.

"Negative, *Uller*," *Jouster* responded. "Boss wants the fear of the Creator today and clear skies for Phase 2. Only survivors are those that go straight down right now and get planetside ahead of us. Let them go. Everyone else gets splattered unless they can outrun us."

Jouster looked down at the scanner once, adjusted himself in his seat slightly, and watched a missile track outbound from their formation like a lightning bolt.

This wasn't going to take long.

Jessica listened to her crew cheer as high-powered optics picked up the Imperial station hit with a flash of light and escaping air.

"Afolayan," she said as the noise died down, "was that one of ours?"

"Affirmative, sir," the dark man replied, turning to smile at her across the space. "The stealth bird got right on top of them before they saw it. Barn owl got her mouse."

"Good shooting," she smiled.

Around her, the bridge crew was all smiles and cheers. It had been a long time since *Auberon* had been able to take it to the *Fribourg Empire* with this much emphasis.

The logs had shown a few encounters with pirates that ran at the first sign of the *Republic*, plus a few deep space rescues of disabled freighters. Nothing nearly this exciting in years.

In a lower orbit, the two groups of fighters began an elaborate ballet, but one that was a foregone conclusion. A handful of missiles leapt out from her Wing and shattered the enemy's already-weak formation like a glass pitcher of water dropped off of a counter. *Jouster's* pilots swooped in on the suddenly-fleeing Imperial craft like sharks chasing tuna.

"Okay, people," she called across the bridge, "time for us to get to work."

She waited a moment for things to quiet down.

"Navigation," she continued, all business. "Bring us into a polar orbit, low enough to avoid moons, high enough to miss satellites. Scanners, who do we have in the neighborhood? Tactical, begin plotting everything within five light seconds and developing firing solutions. Flight Deck, looks like a few of your birds have damage, but everyone is coming home safe. Prepare for retrieval and lockdown."

Heads went down to boards and fingers danced across controls. The noise dropped down to a low murmur of questions into comm devices and the background noise of the air systems, fighting a losing battle with the rank musk of adrenalin.

The smell of fresh coffee perked up her nose.

Marcelle stood beside Jessica's station with a mug, lid opened to let the brew breathe.

She grabbed it with a smile and took a sip. "You really do spoil me, Marcelle."

The tall woman smiled back and nodded, silently withdrawing and exiting the bridge.

Jessica sipped and watched her crew work.

A light came up on her board from the Science/Scanning Officer, sitting well forward in a quiet corner.

"Commander," Centurion Giroux said, his normally quiet voice alive today with energy, "there is a freighter making a run for Jumpspace that you might find interesting. Her manifest shows the vessel is loaded to the gills with metal bar stock. Mostly steel, but also a variety of fairly rare industrial alloys. Pretty valuable cargo."

"We're not pirates, Giroux," Jessica called across the bridge. She watched his head come up and turn to look at her across the suddenly-silent space between them.

"Aye, sir," he called back with a smile, "but if we're going to be out in deep space, well behind enemy lines for a while, we're going to use up a lot of materials doing maintenance. This and the occasional grain transport would let us run wild over here until we ran out of munitions. Plus, we get to kick an Imperial insurance company in the shins."

Jessica smiled. This crew was developing a great potential for mischief.

Speaking of...

Jessica clicked on the comm. "Engineering, this is the bridge. What is the status of *the bomb*?"

Even she couldn't call it anything else these days.

"Ten degrees below freezing, sir," Moirrey's burr came back almost immediately. "Background radiation detectable, but not dangerous, unless you slept in the freezer with it for a month. She's ready to go, any time you want her."

Jessica looked up and realized that every single face on the bridge was turned, watching her with anticipation, except the marine guard in the corner whose job was professional paranoia. Or utter lack of imagination. Maybe both. Marines were like that.

She scanned back and forth. A few of her people looked down or blushed in embarrassment, but the rest just waited.

Jessica took a deep breath. Her nostrils flared. She smiled a hard, predatory grin back at them.

Up until this moment, this had just been a flamboyant raid, deep into enemy territory. Annoying, but merely a footnote in the overall history of a war that had been going on, spasmodically, for over a century. What she was about to do would guarantee her her own chapter.

Or a hangman's noose. Maybe both.

"Roger that, Moirrey," she said. "Transport the weapon to the forward missile bay and arm her for deployment."

Jessica turned, found the Gunner, Centurion Afolayan staring intently at her. "Secondaries only, Afolayan," she said firmly. "Fire a shot across that freighter's bow. Miss by a reasonable distance. Convince them to heave to. Break. Comm, you also convince them to heave to for boarding. Remind them we're the *Republic*, not pirates, so they will be well treated."

Jessica looked at the big board, ships and moons and flight arcs moving in three dimensions. The big white one, *Auberon*, slowly maneuvered into position over the *Ao-Shun* gravity well, stable in a modified Lagrange point. They had plenty of time, unless someone showed up suddenly.

She would deal with that as she had to.

"*Gaucho*, this is the bridge," she called down to the flight deck. "Round up your boarding company of marines and rendezvous *Cayenne* with *Necromancer* to capture a civilian freighter. Science Officer has the specs. Out."

A green light came on as the Assault Shuttle began to pre-flight for launch. He had apparently been sand-bagging down there. Probably already had a company of assault marines aboard.

That man was insane. Useful, but crazy as a junebug.

Jessica leaned back and enjoyed her coffee.

They were going to say the same thing about her shortly.

CHAPTER XXII

Date of the Republic November 14, 392 Polar Lagrange Point over 2218 Svati Prime

"Commander," the voice called out, "*Auberon* is in position over the pole."

Jessica hadn't been day-dreaming, just sitting back and letting her staff do their jobs. Now it was time for her to do hers.

"Defense Centurion Vanek," she said, voice shifting to a formal mode. This was, after all, going to end up before a Fleet Advocate at some point. Maybe it would be a formality.

Maybe not.

Nina turned and looked at her with a serious face. There had been an entire class at the Academy on Stellar Law that dealt with situations exactly like this. Every one of them had passed it to make it this far in their careers.

Jessica wanted to make sure that nobody else hung with her, if that was what would happen.

"Sir?" Nina said.

"Vanek, you have a firing solution for the experimental weapon. You will fire it into the planet's atmosphere."

"Commander, I refuse to carry out that order," Nina said, speaking as much for the gallery and the history books as for her friends and crewmates. "You are bombing unarmed civilians without provocation."

Jessica nodded. Just like the legal books prescribed. She had a really sharp crew. She was proud of these people, just with what they had accomplished so far.

"Protest acknowledged, Vanek," Jessica continued, "and overridden. You will fire the weapon under my authority and my responsibility."

"Acknowledged, Commander," Vanek said.

Jessica, and the entire bridge crew, watched Nina pushed the button on her board.

Below, Auberon suffered a minor earthquake as the missile rack ejected the weapon and sent it on a terminal glide path, a comet lighting up the polar night.

"Missile away, commander," Nina said with authority.

Jessica nodded.

Everything by the book.

Jessica waited a ten count of utter silence before she engaged the comm.

"Engineering, this is the bridge, you are ship-wide," she said. "Moirrey, please provide a color commentary for the crew as *the bomb* makes her descent."

"Aye, ma'am," the voice responded. The excitement made her accent nearly impenetrable, not that anybody would mind. Most of them knew quite a bit about the bomb nicknamed *Mischief*.

"So, boys and girls," Yeoman Kermode continued with a laugh, "these big scary *Republic* pirates are just sitting up there. They've done blown everything to shits and now whats are they goin' ta do? 'ere now, what's that? A missile of some sort. Dun't recognize it. Some new experimental model? An' what're they going to hit clear up at the north pole?

Jessica nodded and sipped her coffee. Moirrey really should have been on the stage. She had the patter and flow of a stand-up comedian. Theater was in her blood. The crew was hanging on her every word.

"Hallo? What's this? The missile is transmitting all sorts of information in the clear? That's not right. Someone up there must be daft, er a screw-up somethin' fierce. We can see everything is doing. And why the hell is a missile below freezing, anyways? What's up with that radiation count? Is not a nuclear weapon. Even shielded, they's hotter'n'that. Can't nobody do nothing to shoot that damned thing down?"

The whole bridge crew was suffering the giggles at this point. It was like a radio drama playing out as Moirrey changed voices and tones.

"This is not good, people. Friction's causing the ice around whatever that warhead is to start melting. Pressure is starting to go through the roof. Wow.

Ice turned to water that fast. Who builts a silly ting like that? Oh, my. Now she's all steam, sealed up tight like a kettle fer tea. The outside, she's red hot noaw. Danger, danger, danger. Hides the women an children. Is a bomb. OH MY GOD, SHE'S GONNA BLOW!!!!"

Silence.

Jessica had to suppress her giggles. Moirrey understood audience psychology at least as well as she did engineering. Probably better. Her voice faded to just above a whisper.

"That's it? Just goes boom clear up in the stratosphere? What kind o'silly bomb does that? Oh, hey, the winds are picking up the mist and radioactive materials from the bomb and scattering them to the four corners of the world. You don't suppose they did that on purpose, do you? What the hell was that bomb carrying? Oh shit, somebody call the Imperial College of Medicine and gets them here quick-like to detect all this shits before people starts dying? Oh my gods, I feel a fever coming on. SOMEBODY DO SOMETHING!!!!"

Jessica simply could not imagine having an entire ship as silent as mice. And yet, here she was. It was truly a *tour de force*. Maybe she should let Moirrey recruit a small theater company and do radio dramas like this more often.

"We now return you to your regular programming, children. Have a good night." Moirrey's voice was back to normal.

The entire crew erupted in cheers, everyone in earshot on the bridge plus everyone close enough to Moirrey down in Engineering. Jessica imagined it was probably everyone with a comm on, anywhere on the ship.

"*Auberon*, this is Command Centurion Keller," Jessica fought to keep her voice level and professional. She felt like she had just committed graffiti all over *Ao-Shun* with a can of neon-pink spray paint. That was pretty close to the truth. "Flag Centurion, have the squadron rendezvous with the captured freighter at point Theta and prepare for Jumpspace. *Ao-Shun* has been successfully raided. Good job, people. Wait until they see what we do next."

Jessica leaned back and glowed. Seriously, there was no better feeling in the world. None.

CHAPTER XXIII

Date of the Republic November 16, 392 Jumpspace outbound from 2218 Svati Prime

Fresh, steaming-hot tea was a wonderful thing.

Denis sat in the officer's wardroom and thought deep philosophical thoughts into his tea. Across the table, he watched Keller devour some sort of stew the cooks had worked up for her.

The menu had changed along with the change in command. Kwok had always paid to have his own personal chef cook meals for him alone, or occasionally a few honored guests and lackeys. The crew ate basic naval rations, unless they paid for something better.

The recipes now were simpler fare, often a meat dish in stew or soup, or occasionally rice. But much better quality.

It was just one of the things that had changed for the better.

"Jež, you awake?"

Denis blinked. "Hmm?"

"I asked if you had enjoyed the ride down on the Flag Bridge," Jessica apparently repeated.

Where had his mind been? *Oh, right. Food.*

"Well, enough, sir," he replied neutrally. He kept forgetting that she paid attention to absolutely everything around her. Another improvement over the previous regime. Probably.

Keller stopped eating long enough to spear him with a hard look.

He shrugged, unwilling to commit further at this point without more of a clue as to what she was about. *Not a woman to play poker with.* But he knew that already.

"Good," she said after a beat, "because I plan to spend my time down there on the next few raids. I just needed to see how this crew responded to stress. And to solutions that didn't come straight out of the standard tactical manual."

"Really?" Denis asked, forgetting all decorum for a moment in his surprise. Kwok had never been content being out of shouting range of everyone on the bridge. "Sir."

She smiled and went back to her food, shoveling in a couple of quick bites.

"And I plan to take Enej Zivkovic down there with me and make him the permanent Flag Centurion," she said after a swallow. "Strnad and he both passed with flying colors when I threw them into the deep end of the pool, so Zivkovic will handle Flag Communications and she can go back to being Tactical Officer. Afolayan will probably need some advanced training to knock off the sharp edges from the Academy, and I think Tamara would be fantastic at that job. You've trained her well."

Denis felt a blush creep up his neck. Yet another difference with Kwok. *Was the rest of his career going to be making comparisons between good officers and Kwok and his predecessors? That would be a nice trade.*

"Thank you, sir," Denis finally managed to get out.

He thought for a moment as she went back to her food.

"I'm surprised at Brewster's change of heart," he said, dangling a bit of bait out there to see what response he would get. *Maybe she was feeling benevolent.*

All he got back was a raised eyebrow. *And maybe she wasn't.*

"He made his choice," she said simply.

Her tone didn't sound like he was dancing on thin ice with his question. He still didn't know her well enough to know the danger signs conversationally.

Denis did know there were things not written in Brewster's personnel file. He had checked.

"Apparently so, sir," Denis replied. "He has so far completed just over one third of the re-qualifications necessary to sit bridge-duty again as a gunner. There have also been a significant drop-off in rumors and whispered complaints about his behavior."

A pause. A breath. Nothing.

"What did you threaten him with?" Denis whispered. "Nobody has ever been able to get him to behave."

Keller stopped chewing and put her bowl down silently on the table. Denis sat perfectly still as she sized him up. And apparently decided he passed.

She leaned forward conspiratorially and smiled. "I threatened to make him a fleet-wide laughingstock, Jež. You don't deal with bullies by challenging them. They thrive on that."

"Oh?" Denis inquired.

"No, you laugh at them, and get everyone else to laugh at them. Nothing deflates a bully faster than being laughed at by everyone. Especially a woman."

"I see," he said.

This woman just kept getting more interesting.

And more dangerous.

CHAPTER XXIV

Imperial Founding: 170/11/26. Xi-Shi

Emmerich sat alone in his office, reading a letter from his youngest daughter, Heike, and sipping an early evening glass of port from his family estates. She was a lovely girl, the apple of his eye, and the child most like him.

Already she was near the top of her class at University. Had she been born a boy, she would have made a fantastic Fleet officer.

A knock at the door a moment before it opened. Captain Baumgärtner shadowed the threshold, holding a handful of printouts in one hand.

"I have anticipated your order, Admiral," he said as the door closed, "and brought the task force to alert."

"How bad is it, Hendrik?" Emmerich said as he sat down the letter and took the bundle from the man's outstretched hand. He nearly dropped his wine as he read the report.

"The *Republic* has executed a raid on *Ao-Shun*, Admiral" Emmerich's Flag Captain said quietly. "They destroyed all of the defenses, and then did, *something*, to the planet itself. Local scientific research has been inconclusive."

"Who do we have in the neighborhood that can help?" the Admiral asked as he continued to read.

"There is nobody available except us, sir," the aide replied.

Emmerich cursed under his breath as the extent of the damage became clear. "Nothing?"

"No, sir. This is the frontier. Each planet generally maintains a squadron of older model fighters as a defensive shell, two if they are closer to *Aquitaine*. That is normally sufficient against pirates."

"Yes," Emmerich agreed, reading the document again. "But this goes well beyond piracy. Order the task force to *Ao-Shun,* immediately. Detach one of the frigates and send it to the local fleet base at *Ashadha* with everything we know and have them send a resupply ship to meet up with us. They will be responsible anyway, but we'll have to hold the fort until they get organized."

Emmerich continued to scan the report.

"Do we know who did this?" he asked.

"According to our spies," Hendrik replied, "it is the woman Aquitaine considers the Hero of *Iger*, Jessica Keller."

"The captain of the escort force?" Emmerich could not hide his surprise. "The one that destroyed *Black Widow*?"

"The same, Admiral," the aide said. "She has apparently been given command of a Strike Carrier Task Force. *Ao-Shun* appears to have been her first target."

Emmerich finally found the brief bio on the woman at the back of the report. Imperial Intelligence had very little information. Just a picture.

She looked remarkably like his youngest daughter.

CHAPTER XXV

Date of the Republic November 28, 392 Jumpspace outbound from 2218 Svati Prime

The coffee was almost cool. But the immense stack of paperwork was almost gone, so it was a fair trade.

Jessica's door chimed once, announcing a visitor. She looked at the clock, rubbed her eyes, and finished her coffee.

"Enter," she called.

Marcelle stood at the door with a serious face. "Are we intruding?"

We?

"No," Jessica replied. "I needed a break."

Marcelle entered, followed by Moirrey Kermode and Nina Vanek, both carrying engineering notebooks. *When had paper gotten back into vogue, rather than electronic storage?*

The four looked at each other awkwardly for a few seconds.

"They were not sure," Marcelle began, "if they should interrupt you with their doodlings, so they came to me, instead."

Jessica looked at each woman closely. "I see. And?"

"And I brought them here, boss," Marcelle smiled. "Don't know the first thing about engineering specifications, ma'am, but I do understand mischief."

She and Jessica smiled at a shared secret. Mischief of that sort was exactly why certain young officers fresh out of the Academy were generally assigned a more-experienced yeoman. It kept them out of trouble. For the most part. Assuming the yeoman wanted to. Sometimes they even did.

Sometimes, they stayed with you for your whole career, creating all sorts of opportunities for more mischief.

Jessica smiled and nodded. "I see. Thank you, Marcelle," Jessica pointed to the two women and the two chairs as her Yeoman exited the room quietly. "Sit."

She studied the two women closely in the silence.

Nina Vanek had a fire in her eyes, and a sureness, a calmness, that had not been there before. She carried herself more and more like Tamara Strnad every day. That alone would be a wonderful outcome of her time here.

Beside her, the little engineering pixie fairly bounced with energy. *No, not a pixie. Perhaps a sneaky, little gnome. Yes. The evil, engineering gnome. They were up to something. And it must be good.*

"So," Jessica said, "it was impressive enough to get Marcelle's attention. What do you have?"

She watched the byplay as the two women glanced at each other.

An entire conversation passed without a word being spoken. Just shrugs, nods, and eyebrows.

"Emperor Napoleon," Nina began, "was able to do much of what he did because he was willing to live off the land, rather than be limited by the efficiency and length of his own logistics train."

Jessica leaned back and considered what she had said.

It was a bold opening gambit. Apparently, today was to be Socratic lessons. Well enough.

"And he failed," Jessica said. "He destroyed his army, his empire, and his legacy, first in Russia, and later against a man who did understand logistics, Arthur, Duke of Wellington."

"Aye, ma'am," Moirrey interjected. "The Iron Duke were a terrible great man, willing to learn new ways of warfare and use patience like water wearing down rock. But he ne'er stepped beyond his supply capabilities. This be the future."

"Go on," Jessica nodded.

"We have cut our own supply chain," Nina continued, "and thrust deep into enemy territory like a saber in the *Valse d'Glaive*. Wellington would have us retreat back to safe territory and plunge in again, somewhere else.

Napoleon would call us cowards and demand that we strip the very land to feed ourselves as we march."

"And why, Centurion, would Wellington be wrong about that choice?"

Jessica felt the energy radiating from the two. It was infectious.

"Because, ma'am," Moirrey replied with a smile, "t'would be the classical response. The book answer. An' we're no about the book."

"No?" Jessica asked.

"No, commander," Nina continued. "We have already proven that we can capture raw materials like metals and food stuffs as we go, and sustain ourselves in the field for a very long time. *CR-264* was designed for amazingly long sails, although *Rajput* will be a cramped pain in the arse after a few months."

"Go on," Jessica said. These two were up to something. She would sell them rope for a while. They had earned her patience. Especially after *2218 Svati Prime.*

"So, eventually," Nina said, "we run out of interesting stuff. Missiles, electronics, reloads for the Primaries. At that point we have no choice but to head home. During that time, the Imperials will gain space to fortify and rebuild everything. When we come back, it will be that much harder to do anything to crack that nut. And we run the risk of running into a force we can't thrash."

"That is essentially correct," Jessica replied. "We do not have the resources to capture one of these worlds, unless you think fifty-eight marines could do the trick?"

"No, ma'am," Moirrey leapt into the fray, "but we could make it right bloody expensive fer them to do anything while we're gone. Like you said, this is a war on their pocketbooks and their minds, not just their navy."

"And how would you two go about doing that?" Jessica finally asked after studying each woman in turn.

"Minefields," Nina said quietly.

"Minefields?" Jessica blinked in surprise. She had expected something else. Something bigger. Stranger.

But as she thought about it, she realized it worked. She had tasked these two women with mischief. This was mischief in spades.

"Aye, ma'am," Moirrey smiled broadly. "We can capture missiles from the Impi's, but we can't really use them. Too much effort to try to reprogram them, wrong diameter, wrong launch rails. That sort of thing. But we can take the boom-stuff out and make more bombs out of them. Real booms this time, an' not just gravel we've irradiated in the landing bay to make a Geiger counter chirp and a bunch of ice to make a nice messy splatter on the scanners."

Jessica pointed to the sketch books. "I see you've given this a lot of thought. Convince me."

Nina smiled and flipped hers open to the first page.

"This," she said, "looks like a standard Imperial communications satellite, because we build it to look just like one, and stuff if with a small engine to make terminal maneuvers, and enough explosives to kick a cruiser's shields in…"

CHAPTER XXVI

Imperial Founding: 171/01/06. 2218 Svati Prime

This was one of the downsides of command.

Admiral of the Red Emmerich Wachturm, resplendent in full dress uniform, sat at the far end of the conference table and listened to the local Governor continue his profanity-laced tirade, all the while attempting to keep a neutral face himself.

It was getting difficult as the man worked his way to a full head of steam.

Still, better to let him vent it all out now. He would be less likely to take it out on someone else, someone who had no choice but to listen.

"And just where was the Fleet when we needed you to protect us?" the man peaked, slamming a perfectly manicured fist down on the table with just the right amount of theatrical flourish. It was astoundingly-well done for a provincial governor in a fringe province.

Emmerich waited for him to settle into a scowl and picked up a piece of paper from the stack in front of him. He quietly read the eleven names on the piece of paper aloud, slowly, solemnly.

When he was done, Emmerich replaced the piece of paper on the stack and smiled a tired, hard smile back at the man.

"Who were those men?" the Governor sneered.

Emmerich paused for a beat. Several aides had the courtesy to suddenly look pained.

"Those were the eleven Imperial Fleet pilots who died defending your world. One man managed to escape by diving into the atmosphere ahead of the raiders."

"That coward should have fought to the death as well," the Governor snarled.

"Really?" Emmerich asked.

He considered his day, his mood, his companion.

Yes, perhaps he had had enough of this little shit. Perhaps he should make an example of him.

"Given that logic, Governor, so should you."

"What? Do you know who I am?" the Governor snarled, obviously forgetting where he was, and who.

"No," Emmerich smiled sadly at the little man. "But I shall be sure to ask my cousin, the Emperor, next time I see him. Perhaps he should know who you are."

Emmerich's smile turned as cold as liquid nitrogen.

He watched the two aides on either side of the Governor turn white as sheets and shudder involuntarily. The Governor himself recoiled as though he had been slapped, although, given what Emmerich knew about the man, he was most likely to be slapped by extremely young women vainly attempting to resist his sexual advances.

"The Fleet is here now," the Admiral continued, building to his own peak. An hour of listening to these pip-squeaks rant had honed his mood down to a fine, sharp edge. Perhaps it was blade-in-the-night time. "We will protect *2218 Svati Prime* until a new fighter squadron can be deployed."

"It won't be enough," the man challenged.

Truly, the Governor had an overwhelming sense of his own importance.

Perhaps the Imperial Taxation Authority needed an anonymous tip. A man with that big of a chip on his shoulder was certain to be doing something that could get him arrested and gulaged, somewhere really interesting.

Perhaps a world farming ice worms would do.

"Then, Governor," Emmerich continued, raising his voice a notch louder to speak over the man, "perhaps we should discuss raising the rate of Imperial Taxes you pay, to afford a better defensive array. I suppose we could always annex the world to the Imperial Estates. Then the costs would be borne by the Household itself. Of course, we wouldn't need a local Governor. What do you think?"

Apparently, the Admiral's tone had finally gotten the man's attention, gotten him to listen to the words.

Emmerich watched him subside like a failed soufflé and sit quietly.

Finally.

"That won't be necessary, Admiral," he said meekly.

"Are we sure?" Emmerich asked, using the tone that he would normally use on an unruly teenage daughter. He had had enough practice.

"Quite sure, sir."

Emmerich let the room stew for a few moments. The sudden musk of fear and flop sweat from the far end of the table, while gratifying, was sour, and threatened to take his mood with it.

"In that case, Governor," he said, "that will be all. I will meet with the medical and scientific authorities next and determine the best course of action. My staff will be in touch."

The aides popped out of their chairs like groundhogs hearing a predator. The Governor rose more slowly.

"I should be here," the Governor said meekly. "This is my world."

Emmerich looked harshly down his nose at the man. He invoked that particular voice of doom he had learned from his father. "This is my world, governor. Until I say otherwise. Are we clear?"

"Yes, sir."

Cattle prods and a stampede of wild bulls couldn't have cleared the room faster. And probably would have left him feeling cleaner. He wanted to wash manure off his boots.

Emmerich looked about at his own staff.

"Okay," he sighed, "now bring in the experts."

Emmerich felt his heart sink again.

Every time he watched the video play, it was like a hot needle poking him.

The Aquitaine carrier, *Auberon*, moving into high orbit exactly over the northern pole of *2218 Svati Prime*. Hanging there, ominous.

Waiting.

A single, strange-looking missile launched down into the atmosphere.

On the side of the screen, all the telemetry data displayed in the clear. Someone had apparently forgotten to encrypt the signal on their weapon, which suggested it was an experimental device, rather than one that was ready for service. So much data made it a boon to decipher.

Why field test it on 2218 Svati Prime? What did this world have that made it a good test? What was going to happen next?

Two and a half tonnes of water, according to the calculations, frozen around the payload inside the warhead.

Some sort of mildly radioactive payload itself, although it had been fully dispersed by polar winds long before a scientist could get there to collect samples.

Friction heating the warhead as is dove, a meteor flashing across the sky. Ice almost subliming instantly to steam from the heat. Pressure building to immense levels before the warhead exploded.

A weather satellite had managed to pick up a grainy image of the explosion itself, a burst of water vapor and *something*, several hundred meters across, quickly torn apart by the high-altitude winds.

What the hell was it? *Aquitaine* had never done something like this before. There were rules.

No matter how bad things were, both sides had always honored the Laws of War.

Emmerich made a note to have one of his legal experts research if this constituted a violation, and, if so, what they could do besides complaining to the Republic Representative through unofficial channels.

Even in a war, there were ways.

Did the ice serve to insulate the warhead? Or was it the steam and pressure that created some manner of secondary effect necessary on deployment.

The video faded to black.

Emmerich looked at the two men chosen to represent the medical profession and the local university science department.

They looked like hell.

Partly, he expected that the dread of meeting the Imperial Admiral, who was also the cousin of the Emperor, was wearing on them. It would wear on anybody.

Add to that the trauma of whatever *Aquitaine* had done with that bomb.

He smiled as the room lights came back up.

"So, gentlemen," he said quietly, warmly, friendly, "what do we know?"

The two men were Mutt and Jeff. The Medical Doctor was short, rotund, and near-sighted. The Doctor of Science was rail-thin, very tall, and fidgeted constantly.

The Medical Doctor spoke first.

"There have been no demonstrable illness clusters that we can directly relate to the event," he said tiredly. It looked like he had had about two hours of sleep in the last week.

"However," he continued, "visits to emergency rooms and clinics are up nearly fourteen percent since the news broke. Hospitals are nearly overwhelmed. Thank you, by the way, for sending so much of your Fleet's medical staff down to assist. It has made the workload manageable."

Emmerich nodded. Dealing with professionals was so much more pleasant than politicians.

He turned to the Doctor of Science expectantly. The man flushed with embarrassment.

"Whatever they have done," the man said angrily, "it has managed to evade all of our tests. Everything we could think of has come back negative. So much so that we have pushed the very limits of science and rationality to come up with new theories. Have they done this anywhere else?"

Emmerich shook his head. "They have not," he said. "On the one hand, unfortunate because we don't have any other situations against which to compare. Fortunate, because there is only this one place."

"For now," the Medical Doctor interjected. "While there have been no symptoms, as yet, we should consider the eventuality of enforcing a quarantine on *2218 Svati Prime*, just to be safe."

"It has been nearly two months, gentlemen," Emmerich said. "Even given my limited training, I cannot imagine a bio-weapon or disease that could have successfully hidden itself from all of modern medicine, and then would break out suddenly enough to be a threat. We will continue to be careful, but I do not think that is necessary. What else?"

"Reports of greater than normal aurora borealis have come in from everywhere," the scientist said. "Again, nothing that stands up to scrutiny, but the general populace is not particularly mollified by scientists telling them not to worry. And the Governor is a populist with an anti-scientific bent."

"Please let my staff know if the Governor presents any problems or impediments to your work," Emmerich noted dryly. "I look forward to addressing them if they do. Personally."

The two men blinked at him, and then glanced at each other. Emmerich could see evil grins begin to grow, carefully hidden.

"What else?" he said.

"If you will turn to page 184," the scientist began…

CHAPTER XXVII

Date of the Republic February 4, 393 Edge of the C'Xindo system

Time to get to work.

Jessica smiled as the scanner board came live and everyone on the Flag Bridge engaged.

Auberon's Pilot, Nada Zupan, had dropped them exactly on target, two light hours out from the Imperial Sector Capital and well above the plane of the ecliptic. *CR-264* and *Rajput* dropped into space right behind them.

Even here, the area was crowded. Several signals indicated sensor buoys lighting up as the squadron were located. The squadron would be identified in fairly short order, but Jessica's plan involved them only staying here for exactly six minutes, just long enough to get a good image of the planet, and they would outrun the news of their arrival.

The Flag Bridge was smaller than the main bridge, down a deck and tucked in closer to the ship's core. There was a big holographic projector in the middle of a conference table, plus space for the squadron's various commanders to be projected if they weren't physically present. Most weren't.

Right now, Jež's electronic image sat across from her, between Command Centurion Alber' d'Maine on the bridge of *Rajput* and Command Centurion Tomas Kigali aboard *CR-264*.

Her Science Officer, Daniel Giroux, was also present via image, tucked into his corner of the bridge. Right now, he was furiously pushing buttons and dialing gauges as he worked to absorb all the information the sensors were bringing in.

The only other person physically present at the table with Jessica was her Flag Centurion, although a few other crewmembers sat at duty stations around the outside of the room, ready to step in or answer questions as necessary.

Jessica studied the image before her, watching fuzzy edges refine quickly as data came into real-time from rough calculations.

C'Xindo was a normal world. It was half green and half blue, reflecting a mix of continents and oceans, but otherwise unremarkable. It had been colonized thousands of years ago, during the Concord Era, but largely lost during the Crash.

In the thousand-odd years since humans had rediscovered starflight and expanded outward, it had been functionally recolonized, growing enough to make it a sector capital when the *Fribourg Empire* pushed its boundaries this far.

Useful, habitable stars were thin out here, but neither *Fribourg* nor *Aquitaine* had put in much effort. *C'Xindo* had a population of around forty million, mostly farmers, with only a few cities, none of them large, or impressive, or interesting.

It did have a nice space station in orbit that served as the Governor's Official Residence and Palace. Between that and being the sector capital, it was better protected than *2218 Svati Prime* had been.

That was one of the reasons Jessica had avoided making it the first target. It was more fun letting the fringe worlds panic and demand protection that might normally have to come from here. Maybe, just maybe, someone had made a mistake and stripped the local cupboard bare.

One could hope.

She turned to her Science Officer as a large signal in orbit near the Palace appeared in the image.

"Giroux," she asked, "what is that?"

"Working," he said, not even looking up.

"That, commander," came the voice of *CR-264's* Command Centurion, Tomas Kigali, "is an Imperial BattleTug. Probably the old *Langschwert*, given the location."

"Really?" she said with surprise. "I haven't seen one of them since Second Year Tactics Class."

Kigali shrugged. He was a tall blond man, thin and rakish. She knew he had set records in a personal yacht for distances sailed and navigational accuracy. He was a perfect fit for a long-sailing, up-gunned Revenue Cutter that might spend years in space between refits.

"They don't have many, and that's the only one I know of on this frontier," he replied. "Normally they guard important military installations. Maybe someone over there was a touch frightened?"

"Can we take him?" Jessica cast into the group.

The other Command Centurion, d'Maine off of *Rajput*, spoke up. He was a dark-complected man, generally dour and serious. Also a good fit in command, for a cramped heavy destroyer that didn't like to make epic voyages.

"Depends on if their Captain's any good," he muttered. "Firepower like a battlecruiser on a good day. Maneuverability of a small planet. We get the drop on him and get out fast, should be doable."

"Since we don't have a bomb to hit the planet with this time, my plan doesn't change, gentlemen," Jessica announced. "Hard and fast. We'll launch everything, make one solid strafing run, and then run for the edge of the gravity well. Depending on how it goes, we may circle back for more, or we may just flit out and go hit the next target. If the BattleTug is here, he's not anywhere else, and we'll get anywhere faster than that old tub could."

She considered the layout of the world. The BattleTug was in a higher orbit and moving faster than the station. They might even be able to catch the two on opposites sides of the planet from each other, pick one, and hammer it while ignoring the other.

"Gentlemen, your orders," she said, making eye contact with everyone once as she spoke. "*Rajput* in the van, with *CR-264* flying close escort on the lower flank. Auberon will come in behind. We'll time the heavy fighter craft to make their pass when you do. The melee fighters will either escort *Auberon*, or close with the strike, depending on what the Imperials do. Questions?"

"What happens if someone is disabled, sir?" Kigali asked.

"If you or *Cayenne* can rescue them safely, we'll do so," she replied. "Otherwise, they get to be prisoners of war for a while, until the next exchange. This is just a raid. And the fourth one of these. What we're up to does not constitute an invasion, as much as they might think otherwise."

"Roger that," Kigali said, his image blanking out as he prepared to transition his ship back to Jumpspace.

CHAPTER XXVIII

Date of the Republic February 4, 393 C'Xindo system

Jouster launched first when they came out of Jumpspace. It was his Flight Wing, his people, his rules. And he would lead by example. Even for crazy people like Commander Keller.

He did one fast visual scan in all directions as he emerged from the bow of *Auberon*, checking visually for trouble instead of just relying on his instruments and sensors. It was the best habit have, out here on the sharp end of the stick.

Across the keel of the carrier, *da Vinci's* P-4 *Outrider* launched simultaneously.

Her scout fighter was built up from the same hull design as his M-5 *Harpoon*, but with only the single Type-1 weapon forward on the nose instead of his triple mounts that parallaxed.

It was a scout, not a melee fighter. One of her reactors and both missile rails had been pulled, for the bulb of a scanner poking out like a pregnant belly underneath.

They always launched this way, the two of them leading the way. He accelerated forward slowly, knowing she would do the same. Behind, the rest of the wing and the big Gunship would be pouring out into space, down the launch rails or out the bay doors.

It's what Strike Carriers did. Get in close, drop enough mobile firepower on the target to take on a battlecruiser, and go to town.

Time to party.

A blue light appeared on the console in front of him. That would be *Auberon* telling him that everyone was launched and away. He waited for confirmation from his people.

"*Jouster*, this is *Southbound*," Marta Eka's voice came over the comm. "All three Wings are forming up now."

Jouster smiled and glanced back over his shoulder at all the lethal metal strung out. Strike Carriers were supposed to send out three flights in a curve, with the Command Wing in the center and the other two back and on each flank. They were also supposed to be flying nine fighters of the same type.

On Auberon, pilot, we do things different. Learn them if you want to survive.

His Wing was on the left, his two wingmates, *Uller* and *Vienna*, stacked above and behind him like stair steps. Over and nearly at the edge of vision, he could see *Southbound* coming into the same position, with *Ironside* and *Bitter Kitten* layered back. Between them, *da Vinci* appeared almost lonesome, until you looked farther back and saw the two big S-11 *Orcas*; slow, armoured, medium-assault saturation bombers, and the even bigger and meaner Gunship, *Necromancer*.

Imperials coming at them were always expecting opponents on the same plane as them. Facing a wall of fire was just one more way to throw them off.

And it worked.

"*Jouster*, this is *da Vinci*," came the call. "*Rajput* and *CR-264* are out front and confirm *Auberon*'s signal. Defenders agree with the previous estimate, with one notable exception. Somebody brought a BattleTug to the dance."

"Are we still targeting the Palace?" he started making adjustments to follow the line *Rajput* was taking ahead of them, and come in over the top at maximum speed for a surprise.

"Affirmative, *Jouster*," the scout pilot responded. "That Tug got caught pants around ankles."

"Squadron, this is *Auberon*," came the call from the new Flag Centurion. "Apparently, today was some local holiday celebration. It appears from the unsecured comm traffic that a great many important people were over at the Palace and are trying to get home now. Consider anything that moves a target of opportunity to decapitate multiple targets, as scanners show a number of small, private yachts docked at the station. Happy hunting."

Jouster smiled. It would be total chaos down there if the station had to positively identify every target before shooting at it, especially at the speed they would be coming through.

That gave him an idea.

"*da Vinci*," he said, "what's the tug doing now?"

"Stand by," he heard her respond.

On his scanner, *Jouster* watched a pair of defense fighters moving in to land on the station instead of moving out to engage them.

They hadn't been loaded with fireworks instead of missiles, had they? Not ready to actually fight? Awful bad planning on someone's part, if that was the case.

Up ahead, the scanner lit up as *Rajput* sent six missiles downrange in as many seconds. *CR-264* moved below her into a proper escort position, and began to engage inbound missiles from the station and a small escort gunship sitting nearby in a defensive position.

Nobody had expected party crashers today.

"*Jouster*," *da Vinci* came back to him. "Tug's engines were cold and are just firing up now. She will be unable to change orbits to catch us coming out with anything but long range deflection shots. Suppose they're good enough to go Parthian on us?"

Didn't these people know there was a war on? Hadn't we hit enough planets along the frontier to get the news out? Was he ever going to get an opportunity like this again?

"*Southbound*, this is *Jouster*," he smiled like a fox contemplating an unlocked hen house. "Continue on your regular run. Escort the Saturation Wing in and engage targets of opportunity."

"Affirmative, *Jouster*," he heard *Southbound* say with a tired, exasperated sound. Was he that predictable? "Couldn't resist, could you?"

Apparently he was.

"*Uller* and *Vienna*, I am transmitting a new course. Form on me and prepare to make a strafing run on the BattleTug."

Jouster felt like a hawk as his group spun up and away. From this distance, it wouldn't take much to come left of the planet instead of right. The Palace would be chasing them even as they chased the tug.

"Flight Wing, this is *Auberon*," came the voice of doom. Keller really was listening in, wasn't she? Kwok would have been having tea somewhere, possibly while being entertained by one of the enlisted crew.

"Your orders were to engage and cripple the station and her defenders," Keller said succinctly. "Return to your original course."

"*Auberon*, target is well in hand," he replied with a smirk. "This is more chaos to sow."

He expected one more threat. Something like *I'll have your head*, mister, but she fell silent. Kwok would have blustered some more.

Keller didn't bluster.

So, he just had to come home a hero and she wouldn't be able to touch him.

After all, she had done the same, hadn't she?

Jessica stopped before she got really going grinding her teeth. She should have known *Jouster* would do something like this eventually. The man was just too much a cowboy.

Enej looked up from his Flag Centurion station with concern. "Orders for the Flight Wing, sir?"

Jessica got out of her seat and walked around the projections. It was just as easy to spin it in place from her command chair, but this forced her mind into new positions. She often saw things not readily apparent when she did it this way.

Jouster was about to get into the hornet's nest, and she had no intention of taking the whole squadron down into melee with a BattleTug, regardless of how off-line the ship claimed to be. She would have been playing possum right now, hoping someone was stupid enough to get into range so they could get bit.

"Private signals, with acknowledgements, Flag," she said, pacing. "Remind *Southbound* that she's in command of the Flight with *Jouster* running off and ignoring orders. Tell her to be ready to come to *Jouster's* rescue if things go bad. Remind *CR-264* to shift sides as they come around the horizon above that tug, so *Rajput* has clear shooting. If that thing gets mobile, they are both outgunned, even if we came in above. Suggest to Jež that *Auberon* drift lower so we can up into the BattleTug's belly if we have to. We'll be climbing out of the gravity well, anyway."

She watched the young man type furiously and then look up at her. "Messages away, Commander."

"Okay, Enej, Blue Team/Gold Team exercise. You command the BattleTug, in the given scenario. What do you do?"

She watched him bring up a local projection at his station and spin it to put him on the far side.

"If I'm pulling an ambush, I light the engines and come barreling around the planet right about now," he said. "That puts me right into *Rajput* as she comes clear of the station. Hit her at close range with the Type-2's, just enough to tickle her. Hold the Type-1's for point defense and smacking fighters around if they get too close. Ignore *CR-264* as she passes. Hold the Primaries and the Type-3's for *Auberon* and pull a fencing pass trying to gut us. The Gunship running with the fighters would be an ugly surprise, especially if the S-11's decide to ignore the station and hit me with everything they have. But I don't believe you'll see me coming in time to have the fighters hold back firepower for me."

Jessica considered the options and the physics of the situation.

"I like it," she said. "Have Jež launch a probe over the pole and have it transmit the BattleTug's location when we drop into the planet's sensor shadow. Tell *da Vinci* to listen for that scenario and prepare to shift targeting accordingly."

"Aye, sir," he said. "Not what you expect?"

She considered the young man. Brilliant tactician, but lacked the killer instinct. Good at multi-level chess, needed to learn how to get creative.

"I can't imagine a fifty-year old BattleTug orbiting for the party had her primary crew in command. Everyone important would be at the dance. We have the second string people. Younger, and less predictable, but also less likely to take decisive action when surprised like this. The Empire keeps a close reign on command authority."

"I see. So what would a young Centurion do?"

"They call the rank *Lieutenant*, Enej," she said quietly, reliving the same conversation with Kasum more than a decade ago. "The book says to bring everything live and wait for the Captain, their equivalent of a Command Centurion. With *Jouster* about to come over their butts, they will concentrate everything on him and be waiting."

"And the problem?"

"Look at *Jouster's* course as he plotted it," she said.

"Orbital insertion on the BattleTug's plane of motion," he replied. "Puts him right in place for a good strafing run with maximum exposure before they break out and climb up the gravity well to escape."

"Yes," she said. "Tactically sound. What happens if the Flight Commander over there sees it and realizes they can chase *Jouster* down way easier than they can chase us, given our head start and their relative motion in orbit."

"Oh. Is there anything we can do?"

Jessica returned to her chair and settled in to sip her coffee. "I have no intention of getting *Auberon* into melee with a BattleTug, especially since *Rajput* and *CR-264* are already committed on their run. *Jouster's* on his own."

Jouster was feeling really good about himself. *Uller* and *Vienna* were sitting stacked above and behind him. The BattleTug's crew had apparently gotten themselves back on line and were trying to make it to the party, if only a little late. *Auberon* had even launched a probe so they could see the whole situation without having any blind spots.

This was how you were supposed to fight a war.

He watched on his scanners as *Rajput* hammered the living shit out of the Palace as she flew past, taking barely enough counter-fire to even count. The rest of the Flight Wing made a pass on the gunship and a couple of defensive platforms, overloading those poor bastards and blowing them out of the skies.

Seriously, he had the best Flight Wing on the frontier, maybe the top three in the fleet.

"*Jouster*, this is *da Vinci*. Watch your six."

Jouster watched as she highlighted a new signal on his scanner.

Shit. Who told them they could do that?

Five Imperial fighters had launched late and simply ignored everything else. Now they were on his ecliptic and pouring around the edge of the planet at him from behind. At full speed.

He did some quick math. If he slowed down to engage them, they might miss the rendezvous point.

Would Keller leave him here? She had threatened too.

If he sped up, they would barely get a shot at the tug in passing, hardly enough to even warm up their shields, certainly not enough to do any damage.

Imperials weren't that good, were they?

Can't turn and launch missiles at them from here without getting trapped. Nothing I can do now but run with my tail between my legs.

"*Uller. Vienna.* Prepare to come to red-line speed. We've got to try to outrun them."

Both pilots acknowledged and kept up as he pushed the throttle to the last stop and locked it there. He considered dumping all of his missiles, just to reduce weight and drag on the wispy tops of the atmosphere.

That would look really good on the after-action report, wouldn't it?

He watched precious minutes tick by. Ahead, the BattleTug was ignoring them, trying to chase the rest of the squadron. Behind, the Imperials slowly caught up, lighter and faster around the curve, and taking a slingshot trajectory. They would only get one shot, but they would have speed and position when they did.

This was going to suck.

Vienna's voice came first. It was just as dark and sultry as she was. Not his type, but she certainly made *Uller's* motor run, even if she would never give him the time of day. "Missiles inbound," *Vienna* said calmly. "Initiating defensive measures now."

Jouster cursed silently. That would just slow them down more at the very time they needed speed to escape.

He deployed his screamers, hot little boxes broadcasting a loud radio signal. Incoming missiles often locked on those instead of the primary target, but he had to back his engines down to be less of a thermal signature.

He banked, climbing up and away from the screamers, just as his wingmates were doing above him.

This was bad. The five Imperials had slowed as well. They might be able to brake enough to engage, instead of blasting right by. And the BattleTug was coming up under them.

He was about to be caught between the proverbial rock and hard place.

Flashes of light marked the impact of Imperial missiles on defensive buoys. At least that much had worked.

And then his defensive systems warbled as the Imperials got a targeting lock.

"Team," he yelled. "Go for broke, straight up. Now."

"Negative, *Jouster*," a female voice interrupted. "Hold your line for six more seconds and then climb out."

That was Lagunov. What the hell was *Bitter Kitten* up to?

Jouster red-lined the engines once more and wobbled his craft back and forth. He could see pulses flash past him as ionized packets of energy missed.

The Imperials were actually close enough to engage with Type-3's? Crap.

Jouster barrel-rolled to the right, careful to stay flat as he did so, but hopefully catching the Imperials out of position. The scanner showed *Uller* and *Vienna* staying right with him. All those hours in the flight simulator were paying dividends right now, as they moved like a school of fish.

"*Jouster*," *Bitten Kitten* called out, "Pull up now."

He pulled back on the yoke and felt inertial forces drive him down into the seat.

He watched two friendly craft slalom right under his formation at full speed, triple cannon firing as fast as the generators could pulse them. He hoped the Imperials were as surprised as he was.

Jouster pulled a quarter rotation pivot as he climbed, leaving the entire battle field above him out the cockpit window. Five Imperials fighters had suddenly turned into two as *Bitter Kitten* and somebody else shot past.

She got three of them?

The other direction, a wall of fire erupted over the dorsal hull of the BattleTug, secondary explosions feeding on each other.

Just as he cleared the gravity well and pushed his fighter over to make the rendezvous with *Auberon*, a flash of light appeared on his scanner.

One of the two fighters who had just saved his butt disappeared in a cloud of fire as a missile slammed into it.

"*da Vinci*, this is *Jouster*," he said quietly. "Who got hit?"

Lagunov answered first. "That was *Ironside, Jouster*. They got Gustav."

So. One of his wasn't coming home. And had died rescuing him from his own stupidity.

There was going to be hell to pay when he got back to *Auberon*.

CHAPTER XXIX

Date of the Republic February 6, 393 Jumpspace outbound from C'Xindo system

Only one chair on this side of the table was occupied, to the two over there.

She was not out-numbered.

Jessica sat in the center of the long table and looked across at her two pilots.

It was not a happy look. She was not a happy woman.

She had, however, left the seats on either side of her empty.

If this was going to be a formal Court of Inquiry, she would have installed two other people as judges, probably Denis Jež and Iskra Vlahovic. Having the First Officer and Flight Deck Commander, her second in command and the air boss respectively, would have meant formal charges. Career-ending sorts of inquiries.

She was not that angry.

Quite.

It was a close thing.

She let the silence hang. Hopefully, Milos Pavlovic, commonly known as *Jouster*, and Darya Lagunov, *Bitter Kitten*, would be able to grasp how angry she was and keep very, very quiet while she stewed over the after-action reports.

She looked up at each of them in turn.

Bitter Kitten had the decency to look embarrassed and sorry, like a school girl who had forgotten to turn in a term paper on time and was waiting for the headmistress to come down on her.

Jouster sat with a scowl on his face, like he really didn't believe he had done anything wrong. In his mind, he might not have. There was a reason he was on the frontier, rather than in the war zones. No commander there had been willing to put up with his shenanigans for long. Even if he was one of the best pilots in the fleet.

However, that only got you so far.

Jessica set the stack of papers down and glanced at the two empty seats at her side.

"I had considered a Court of Inquiry for the actions at *C'Xindo*," she said, quietly enunciating the words.

The two pilots leaned forward a bit to hear her.

So at least she had their attention.

"If it ever happens again, there will be one. And any forbearance on my part now will weigh heavily on the charges filed then. Am I clear?"

Lagunov nodded forcefully. "Aye, sir," she said, "won't happen again."

Pavlovic looked askance at the woman beside him for a moment and scowled harder. He made eye contact across the table. "As you wish, commander."

Jessica fought down the urge to lean across the table and slap him. Scion of one of the bluest of the blue blooded clans. Video-star looks. Pain in the ass because nobody was willing to challenge his family.

Yes, she knew his kind. Knew them from prep school and the Academy, when a poor scholarship student was a second class citizen. When she was expected to shine the boots of officers like him on the weekend. Possibly for tips if the job was well done.

She really wanted to wreak a vast and terrible vengeance upon his head right now, but it would look petty. And it would reflect poorly on her as a commander that things had gotten to this point. It would create unnecessary problems for the First Lord.

She wasn't ready to fight that war.

Yet.

She leaned back instead. She was the senior Command Centurion on this frontier, by right of commanding the largest vessel. She was no Fleet Lord, but there were no Fleet Lords looking over her shoulder here.

She smiled. It was a devious, evil smile.

Bitter Kitten paled. Even *Jouster* blinked.

"All of this will be entered into the formal record," she said. "We will consider this an informal Commander's Mast. Lagunov, you are grounded for the next forty-eight hours and assigned to whatever duty the Flight Deck Commander deems fit during that time. I will suggest to her that you clean the Officer's restroom with a toothbrush. And that will be that. Am I clear?"

"Yes, sir," *Bitter Kitten* nodded and spoke quietly. They both knew it could have been much, much worse.

"Then you are dismissed," Jessica said.

She waited while the pilot stood, saluted, and fled out the door without another word.

Jessica stared back at *Jouster* hard. He had a very hard head and a wide stubborn streak. It had served him well to get this far in life and command. It was time to get through to him, one way or the other.

"*Jouster*," she smiled hard, "you're grounded."

His scowl grew confused. Obviously, not the turn of event he was expecting.

"For how long?" he asked.

Her smile widened, turned feral. "Until I say otherwise. Until you give me a reason to trust you again, or you put in for a transfer to anywhere else."

He shot to his feet. "You can't do this," he thundered.

She smiled up at him, knowing it was digging in deeper than a tick under his skin. "Watch me, *Jouster*. Just watch me."

"I'll fight you on this. Do you know who my family is?"

Now she fought to keep the purr out of her voice. He might be a great pilot, and a fantastic tactician, but he lacked that certain strategic level of thinking.

"If you cross me, *Jouster*," she said quietly, "I'll have you brought up on charges of Cowardice In The Face Of The Enemy and shipped back to *Ladaux* to stand trial."

He reacted as if she had slapped him. A warm, sharp, open-palmed kind of slap.

Jouster was probably already familiar with those from a woman. However, Jessica wouldn't have slapped him if push came to shove. She would have kicked him in the groin first and then stomped on his hands when he went down.

"You'll never make that stick," he whispered.

She rose from her seat. She barely came up to his nose, but she wanted to lean forward so she could whisper back, like lovers. "I don't have to, *boy*," she breathed, hard at him. "Everyone will know that your famous family connections got you off. But the Fighting Lords will know. Your career will be over and you will never fly anything again, except your father's yacht. I promise you that."

"And if I refuse?" his voice started to creep back up in volume. It came out as more of a snarl.

Jessica pulled one of the papers from the stack, spun it around, and slid it across the table. "Sign this transfer request," she murmured. "I'll turn right now and run for *Simeon* or *Kismayo* as fast as *Auberon* will carry us. You'll be gone, and I'll requisition two replacement pilots I can trust. Easy as that."

"Why?" he cried.

"Because you fucked up," she replied. "That was an amateur move, executed by a lazy pilot, just phoning it in. If you can't fly any better than that, then I have no use for you. And I can't trust you to follow orders, so we're going to lose more pilots bailing your ass out of stupid situations unnecessarily. *Ironside* might have died in the line of battle, but you put him there."

She watched him take a breath and control the anger she had been goading him into.

Okay, so self-control was possible for him. There might be hope.

"What do you want from me, Commander?" he said, trying hard to hold the emotion at bay.

"I would like to trust you, *Jouster*," she replied. "And I would like to think that you were a better pilot than you've shown me. Right now, I'm thinking about putting you on *Necromancer* as a Tower Gunner and seeing who wants to try to qualify as a fighter pilot to replace you."

"I can do better," he said, pain starting to edge into his voice.

"Prove it."

"How?"

"Not my problem, pilot. Dismissed."

She watched him stand there, shocked out of rationality. All the blood had drained out of his face.

She couldn't smile. Not when she wanted to scream at him, or hit him, or demote him. Anything to get through to him and make him act like a grown-up, like the officer and gentleman he was supposed to be.

Maybe it was too late for that.

She picked up her papers, stepped around the table, and left him there.

He would find his way. Or he wouldn't.

CHAPTER XXX

Date of the Republic April 8, 393 Ladaux

His ancient, ornate desk had been made from oaks harvested for the purpose on *Anameleck Prime*. It was so much larger and heavier than the one he had in his office up at Fleet HQ in orbit, but it was a comfort to Nils Kasum as he considered his response to the ornate and heavy piece of linen paper sitting before him, just delivered to his office by an official Senate Messenger.

Had it been in regards to anything other than Keller, the summons most likely would have reached him through normal channels, and he could have dealt with it quietly.

Instead, somebody, probably one of Loncar's friends, had managed to get the Question Of *Ao-Shun* on the Senate's Order of Business and demanded a public hearing, today, on the potential charges of War Crimes Against Humanity.

This sort of move had Loncar's fingerprints all over it. The man was smart and powerful, and absolutely, absolutely as hidebound as they came.

Nils read the page again.

My, such a big sounding, important concept.

He could visualize Loncar seated with someone like Tesar, cuddled up in one of their favorite clubs, whispering conspiracies to each other. Perhaps the very Club down the street where they were all three life members.

Brandy snifters filled with the most expensive vintage. Lights low to further the mood of conspiracy. Wait-staff hired for looks and discretion, rather than competence.

Nils never attended that one. He much preferred the Officer's Bar at Fleet Headquarters, where he could drink and dine with Fighting Lords, and occasionally drop in on younger officers and take their measure.

Yet another reason to stay in orbit as much as possible.

So, a Senatorial subpoena to *Appear And Give Testimony*. It was only proper. The Senate was the final authority on such matters, well within their rights to demand accountability from the Fleet. It was his prerogative as First Lord of the Fleet to defend his people.

If only he could tell them the truth.

Nils reached down and re-opened the closed folder marked *First Lord: Eyes Only*.

Inside, the title page pretty much said it all.

Project Mischief.

He thumbed through a variety of pages, carefully detailed and annotated, and made a mental note to have Kamil dig up the personnel file for one Yeoman Moirrey Kermode and figure out exactly how she had slipped through the cracks to end up where she was. That woman had talent. And a wicked, wicked sense of humor.

When he had sent Jessica Keller to the *Cahllepp Frontier* to cause a ruckus, he had never imagined this. Well, not exactly this.

Still, it had worked, hadn't it?

He checked the time and rose. He had long enough to get into his formal robes and have a bite. It was likely to be a long afternoon.

Hopefully it would be a fruitful one.

Nils took the measure of the great chamber as he entered, announced at the door by the Orator and escorted to his seat by the Sergeant at Arms. The room was serious, but not overly hostile. About normal, all things considered.

A row of Senators on their dais, elevated above the poor victim called to give testimony in the lone seat before them. A gallery of witnesses behind where he would sit, rather full today.

There were too many marriages and alliances interwoven in this chamber for anything like politics to be fixed for any longer than the issue at hand. It was the blessing and the curse of the Republic. Things tended to move slowly, but they had all the maneuverability of a tumbling dreadnaught trying to get the engines back on line. Once events were moving, they kept on a line as straight as a meteor.

Conspiracies like this were nothing new. First Lord of the Fleet was an appointed position, held during the will of the Senate. Appointees usually retired after a time. Rarely did someone get to this level of politics and leave themselves open to embarrassment and censure.

Today, someone in the Senate had thought to sneak up on him, catch him in the gears of state, and grind him into coffee they might serve with dinner? Him?

How quaint.

He smiled at Fleet Lord Loncar, a rare spectacle, seated in the public gallery with a bodyguard, since a serving officer could not sit in the Senate, and he was technically still on active duty, but without a fleet to command.

Besides, his sister was a much better operator anyway. She would have threatened him in a private meeting, so it must have come from some other flank.

Probably her brother. Bogdan was a fool at times.

Well, the truth would come out soon enough.

Nils took his seat before the panel and waited.

The Senate *Select Committee for the Fleet of The Republic of Aquitaine* took itself very seriously.

It's members were all experts on fleet operations and logistics, membership voted on by the body as a whole, rather than subject to a random draw, as some were, or given as favors or sinecure.

Important business like the Fleet was never left to chance.

They were, however, still politicians playing, at least to some extent, to the masses, the mob seated behind him. The text of the prepared statements he had been provided would, at a minimum, require two hours to complete, followed, only then, by questions from the Senators.

That was when things would get interesting.

Nils settled into his chair, alone facing the seventeen Senators on their rostrum, and composed himself to look interested while not falling asleep. That was another acquired skill.

He wasn't that prepared to insult their intelligence. Publically.

Nils could tell by the way the Chairman began to wind his oratory to ever-greater heights that the man was rounding off his prepared statements. It had been entertaining, if predictable. They usually were.

For such a short, pudgy man, he could bring the fire and charisma when he wanted.

So much of what they did was thus. Was that a weakness of the *Republic?* The *Fribourg Empire* could certainly move more nimbly.

Of course, they were far more subject to the whims of a single man.

It was the *Republic's* luck right now to face a competent Emperor surrounded by a stable and experienced staff, working for the good of the *Empire* instead of their own parochial yearnings. At least most of the time.

"So I ask you, First Lord," the Chairman thundered from his seat, "what have you done to investigate the actions of Command Centurion Keller? Why has she not been ordered back to base and arrested for her crimes?"

Nils waited for the mild applause behind him to die down. The Chairman was a natural speaker, but occasionally began to believe his own press releases.

Someone had set the man up today.

However, they had done it in a ham-handed way.

The First Lord glanced sidelong at Fleet Lord Loncar, seated so happily in the front row. Nils would have been willing to bet quite a bit of money that Loncar was behind all of this.

Nils leaned forward and laced his hands under his chin. He put on a serious mien and looked at each of the Senators closely, one at a time.

It was a game of wills.

He was not going to lose today.

Not with these people.

And tomorrow, he would pay them back. He made sure they understood that from the look he gave them.

Most had the decency to look mildly chagrined, or alarmed. Those, he marked down as victims of one of the demagogues on the panel, rather than the instigators.

Finally, he looked backwards over his shoulder, noting that the chamber was open to the public. And someone had paid good money to make sure every seat was full and the mezzanine was packed as well. Standing Room Only.

Normally even the Opening of a Senate every three years wasn't this full.

Nils looked back and around and took the measure of the Chairman.

By now his energy had dissipated and he began to look unsure of himself. It was almost as if Nils wasn't following the script someone had prepared.

Probably gamed it out extensively and convinced themselves they had him boxed in, hadn't they?

Nils smiled at the man. Winter had a warmer kiss.

"Considering," he began, speaking so quietly that the microphone could barely pick it up over the rustle of the observers, "that my office just became aware of the attack on *Ao-Shun* by Command Centurion Keller and the *Auberon* in the last thirty-six hours, we have only now begun to properly investigate it ourselves. I find it interesting that the Senate has apparently been more fully briefed on the matter than the Fleet has."

He leaned back in his chair and let that dangle over people's heads.

He didn't think anyone in the Intelligence Services would be so stupid as to send the Senate reports that didn't also go to his desk, but he was willing to add five or six names on his list for paybacks tomorrow, unless the truth came out sooner.

"So what would you add to this Committee's prepared statements for the record?" the chairman asked.

His voice sounded far less sure of itself than it had a moment ago.

"These sorts of questions are usually asked under seal, Mr. Chairman," Nils pounced, "since Fleet operations against the *Fribourg Empire* are usually handled at the highest level of secrecy. You know, because spies might report things they read in the news. That sort of thing."

My. Quite a number of sour faces over there. Hadn't thought beyond the grandstanding, had we?

"Further," Nils continued, "I would find it interesting to know how such detailed information was delivered to the members of this committee. It certainly didn't come from my office. I learned a few interesting things about the incident just listening here."

Heads were starting to turn towards the Chairman. The looks were less than friendly. Other stares settled in on a frumpy brunette two seats to his left.

Oh, ho. Senator Tomčič, was it? Predictable, I suppose. Often an ally of Loncar and his friends. Usually smarter than this. They must really be upset about Keller and Iger.

"But," Nils stuck the knife in, just a prick, thus far, "since you insist on having this out in open committee, I would ask the assembled Senators, and the Senate as a whole, how you came to be in possession of such a rich file of information, when I, myself, only barely have Keller's reports through a courier, since she, herself, is still out in the field, confronting the enemies of the *Republic* at my command and your behest. Suggestions, Mister Chairman?"

Okay, maybe that knife went in a little deeper than intended. Nothing that couldn't be fixed by a medbot easily enough. If you hurried.

Tomčič looked like she had swallowed the whole lemon, instead of just biting it, like her neighbors had.

And maybe I won't have to exact a bloody vengeance on you people tomorrow, after all. Looks like you'll handle that for me, won't you?

Nils smiled as the Chairman gaveled loudly. The buzz coming from the galleries behind him was getting ugly.

People seemed upset and confused behind him. Something like the senators in front of him.

"Sergeant At Arms," the Chairman bellowed, only audible because his microphone was designed to override anyone else speaking, "Clear the room. This Committee is going into private session."

The noise rose to a roar as the crowd started getting shoved out the way by unfriendly and unforgiving gendarme with shock wands.

Nils rose from his seat amidst the chaos and slipped back into the crowd before the Chairman noticed. He could make it down to his office and have a cup of coffee before they caught up with themselves and realized he was gone.

Next time, they were going to ask very politely for him to join them.

He would make sure of that.

CHAPTER XXXI

Date of the Republic March 7, 393 Qui-Ping system

Hulls glowed dimly in the distant light of the little red dwarf star they were using as a staging base.

Denis stood at the viewport and watched the other ships in the squadron as they orbited the lifeless planet below.

At the center of the resting formation was the cargo freighter they had captured during that first raid on *2218 Svati Prime*, after bombing *Ao-Shun*. They had even kept the name, *Johannesburg VI*, and taken the crew with them to the Fleet base at *Simeon* in December.

That had been an odd trip. Just in station long enough to drop off the prisoners, pick up a skeleton crew to keep *Johannesburg VI* running as a forward base, and enough supplies to stay out another six months. They had even out-run news of their adventures on the Imperial side of the frontier.

"So what do I have to do?" *Jouster* asked from beside him.

Denis had forgotten the man was there as he had stared at the stars below. He turned to *Jouster* now, ignoring the lovely vista behind him.

"You have to convince her, *Jouster*," Denis said quietly. "She's the one that makes that call."

"At least Brewster got an opportunity," Jouster whispered back. They were in a public place right now. Granted, the crew generally left them alone when using the observation dome, but voices would still carry.

"Brewster showed contrition," Denis bit off. "And has worked his ass off since. When have you ever been sorry, *Jouster*? Funny time to be asking for mercy."

"I didn't think she was serious, Denis," the man pleaded.

"She's always serious, Milos," he replied, "the problem is that you never are. Maybe it's time you grew up."

Denis started to say something else when his personal comm beeped. "This is Jež. Go ahead."

Her voice filled the air between the two men. "Denis, could you round up Iskra and Tamara and join me on the Flag Bridge, please?"

"Right away, sir," he replied.

Denis fixed *Jouster* with a glare. "Time for me to go to work. Why don't you go rack up high scores on the simulator on useful missions."

"I already have," came the tart reply.

"I meant on the escort missions, *Jouster*, not the hot-dogging strafe-and-melee missions."

Denis brushed past him, ignoring *Jouster's* surprised face.

Time to go down to the flight deck to grab the Air Boss. Sounded like she had planned another raid.

Denis wondered how many more times they could do this sort of thing before their luck finally ran out, like it had for Gustav Papp, *Ironside*. Eventually, that great gray whale was going to get them.

At least things were never boring.

Denis entered the Flag Bridge last, a step behind the Flight Deck Commander, Iskra. Tamara Strnad was already there, with the Flag Centurion and Keller seated at the table.

He took the last empty seat, between the projections of the other two squadron commanders, warm and snug on their own bridges.

"Ladies and gentlemen," Jessica began, "I'll make this quick. I want us to depart in six hours and make a high speed run to *2218 Svati Prime*. I want to hit them again, at least once, before we head home for rest and refit."

"Any particular reason, Commander?" Denis asked. "By now they've been reinforced."

She nodded in his direction. Not agreeing with him, so much as a placeholder while she organized her thoughts.

"Two reasons," she replied. "First, they have been reinforced, but it's been four months and we've hit a number of other systems along the frontier, each farther from the Imperial Capital and the Home Regions. We haven't gone in a straight line, but planets farther out ought to be on the verge of panic and mutiny by now."

She paused to take a sip of coffee and study the group. Denis watched her and did the same with his tea.

This was the core of what made the squadron so potent. A good group of officers, well in tune with one another, and working to a common goal.

"The second reason," she continued, "is something *da Vinci* picked up at *C'Xindo* on a barely-secured channel. There was apparently a major Fleet Task Force at *2218 Svati Prime* until very recently. The call was a high-ranking politician asking if the force was due at *C'Xindo* soon enough to track us down. The response was garbled, but suggested that they have gone farther down the line to lie in wait for us."

"So, we might have a clear path back, Keller?" Command Centurion d'Maine's ghost asked from next to Denis, echoing his own thoughts. Would it work?

Jessica smiled around the group. It was not a pleasant smile, but Denis hardly remembered her actually smiling much in the last six months since she had taken command.

Had it already been six months?

"I think, considering the circumstances, it might be the very last place they would think to look for us," she said. "However, a savvy and sneaky commander might think those same thoughts and bait a trap for us. We have been pushing our luck, running these raids and only returning to home base once, and then only long enough to pick up a pre-packaged weapon's container full of reloads and supplies."

"Is the enemy commander that canny, sir?" Denis asked, playing a hunch based on her vocabulary. He was starting to learn how she thought. Maybe.

"I believe he is, Denis," she replied. The smile warmed up several degrees. He seemed to be passing more of her unspoken tests these days. Maybe there was hope for him after all.

"The Imperial Admiral is Emmerich Wachturm," she continued. "He was the hero at *Iger*."

Denis had a moment of dis-equilibrium as he watched Kigali's projection lean forward faster than the camera could compensate. It was like bouncing over the top on a roller-coaster for a moment.

"Apologies, sir," he said with conviction, "but I thought *you* were the hero at *Iger*."

Denis watched her smile turn absolutely frigid in an instant. He was glad it was pointed at someone else this time.

"If you want to go there, Kigali," she said quietly, "I might be willing to grant you that I'm the reason we didn't get our asses completely handed to us at *Iger*. What Wachturm did for that battle was a stroke of tactical and strategic brilliance well outside the standard Imperial maneuvers manual we like to deride so much. He should have destroyed us at Iger. He nearly did anyway."

"No offense, ma'am," Kigali verbally backpedaled. He leaned back almost as fast as he had leaned forward, upping the vertigo factor.

Denis was glad he hadn't had lunch yet.

"None taken, Tomas. Just understand that he is the best Fighting Lord they have on their side, hands down. And he's out here somewhere with an Imperial Battleship that outguns this whole squadron all by itself, not counting a half dozen other warships in his Fleet."

"So how do we fight him?" Tamara asked. Denis blinked. She had been so quiet he had forgotten she was there.

Jessica rounded on her hard for a second, and then stopped to take a breath.

"We don't, Tamara," she said. "If he shows up, we run like hell."

"And if we can't?" Tamara continued.

"Then our little adventure is over," Jessica replied.

CHAPTER XXXII

Date of the Republic April 8, 393 Ladaux

By the time he got back to his office Nils was in a slightly better frame of mind. The long walk had ground some of the edges off. Not enough to forget. Maybe enough to forgive. Someone was getting a good yelling at over this.

The only question was who it would be.

Kamil met him at the door with a coffee service for two. It took a moment for the implications to sink in.

"I have a guest?" Nils asked quietly.

"Aye, sir," the man replied quietly. "I took the liberty."

"I see."

There weren't many people that rated that level of service from Kamil, especially when Nils was out of his office. That drastically limited the options. But improved them at the same time. Kamil had very discerning tastes.

Nils opened the door to his inner office and gestured Kamil to precede him in. He followed and found his visitor sitting on the comfortable sofa in the corner, waiting patiently.

Kamil deposited the tray on the desk and looked expectantly at both men.

"We'll take care of it, Kamil," Nils said. "Please see that I'm not disturbed."

"Including the Sergeant at Arms and a company of Gendarme, First Lord?" Kamil smiled sarcastically.

"Make sure they have a warrant first," Nils smiled back and watched the man nod and depart.

Nils turned to his visitor.

The Senatorial robes looked natural on him. He had the air of an actor, with perfect hair and perfect teeth and perfect charm. While he was probably not the single most powerful Senator serving, he was in that handful that made sure things ran smoothly.

"You sit, I'll serve," the man said apologetically. "I invaded your office. It's the least I can do."

So, peace offerings instead of looking for scalps.

Nils moved around the desk and took his seat. It wasn't often that the Premier of the Senate offered to serve you coffee. They both had people for that sort of thing.

"Tadej," Nil began, "what the hell just happened?"

Senator Tadej Horvat, Premier of the Senate, retired Fleet Lord of great note, and owner of a giant ranch filled with prize cattle and chickens, looked at him for a moment and shrugged eloquently.

"I'm not sure yet, Nils," he replied as he sat, holding a delicate cup in one hand.

"I have good people," Tadej continued, "and I pay them well to keep on top of things. They were monitoring the hearing, but hadn't dug deep enough into those reports to realize what was going on. I'll be talking to them next, but I needed to get down here before you did something you wouldn't regret later. Especially since Tomčič is apparently behind it. I know there's no love lost there, especially since *Iger*."

"Tadej, I have brought charges of espionage and treason against people for leaking less sensitive information to the press," Nils sighed.

"I know that," the Premier sighed back. "And I need to keep this from spiraling out of control into an utter scandal. I was all set to go on vacation next week."

Nils smiled. The Premier's vacations were social events of the first order, with people rushing to book up every hotel room in the vicinity, on the off-chance of being seen with him, or, better, being invited to dine and socialize. Marriages were often arranged and fortunes made at such gatherings.

"First order of business will be to slap a highest clearance security rating on that report," he continued.

"I wouldn't bother," Nils replied. "The prepared statements have already gone to the press and there's nothing else in the report that's all that interesting. I would appreciate an explanation."

Tadej sipped his coffee and watched Nils' face. "Calm enough now to ask politely instead of bellowing across the bridge?"

"You planning to be there to referee?"

"I have no choice at this point, Nils. This little stunt is making the Senate look bad. Petty. Silly. School-yard antics. Somebody needs to be taught to handle these things the proper way. That wasn't it."

"Then," Nils said quietly, "I would suggest you read Jessica Keller's personal report right now, Tadej. I wanted to sit on this as long as possible, but I'm not sure that will be possible now. And it makes for such wonderful reading. Especially in light of what went on this afternoon."

He slid the folder across the table and sat back as the man sipped his coffee and flipped through the pages.

Sounds came from him that sounded remarkably like suppressed giggles, but Tadej was far too urbane and sophisticated for that to be the case.

Nils finished his coffee as a knock came at the door.

Kamil opened it a crack, just enough to speak, but not be seen. "First Lord, the Sergeant At Arms is here to see you."

Nils watched Tadej surge out of the sofa angrily. It was like watching a tidal wave suddenly appear on the horizon. He expected the effect would be similar.

The Premier took a moment to very carefully set down his empty mug and the folder before he stomped to the door. Nils smiled as the man took a deep breath and turned on the charm.

Only, it wasn't charm. Planet-crushing anger, perhaps. Lava was certainly involved.

Tadej pulled the door open and confronted a middle-aged man in the formal uniform of the Senate's Gendarme.

"What the hell are you doing here, Milon?"

The anger radiated off of Tadej like heat waves. It was actually a rather fun to watch, since the Premier rarely got the opportunity to use it on people. Nils found it far more entertaining to watch him do it to someone else.

It had the desired effect. From where he sat, Nils could just see the man's face pale and blanch with surprise. He even took a half-step back.

"I was sent by the Chairman, Premier," he stammered nervously. "The First Lord had not been dismissed as a witness and the committee demanded he attend them."

"You work for me, Mister Postovich," Tadej's voice got eerily quiet. "I suggest you return to your office right now and spend some time remembering that. It is a situation I can easily rectify, if provoked. Am I clear?"

"Yes, Senator," the man said, falling over himself in his haste to escape the outer office and colliding with a pair of Senatorial Guards behind him.

The group fled noisily up the hall.

Nils rose as the noise faded. He joined Tadej at the door with a silent look of inquiry.

"Yes, I suppose," Tadej replied. He turned to Kamil. "Thank you for the coffee and the competence. You do a credit to your boss, Kamil, unlike some of my people."

He turned to Nils and sighed. "Let's go put out a fire before it gets further out of hand, Nils."

Nils nodded and trailed into the man's wake.

The afternoon *was* going to be interesting, it seemed.

CHAPTER XXXIII

Date of the Republic March 10, 393 Outbound from Qui-Ping system

Another tactical simulation.

Jessica sat at her desk and went through it, thinking how she would have reinforced *2218 Svati Prime* and, in turn, how to assault that.

Some people knitted. Others read books. This was how she filled her spare time.

It was a seductive game to play, trying to out-think total strangers. Even more so an acknowledged genius of an Imperial Admiral named Emmerich Wachturm. The man so good that the Republic Academy taught him and his tactics.

There was nobody else that had been born in the last century, *Republic of Aquitaine* or *Fribourg Empire*, accorded that honor. Nobody else deserved it.

A knock at the door distracted her. She paused the simulation, then went ahead and shut it down. Her coffee was empty, anyway, so now was a good time to get up and stretch her legs. Maybe another mid-week session with the combat robot.

Valse d'Glaive required subtlety and suppleness in equal measure. It helped to keep her mind from falling into ruts as well, as the robot was programmed to pick up bad habits and exploit them. Often painfully.

"Come," she said, rubbing her eyes.

"You have a visitor, sir," Marcelle said with an odd, subdued tone to her voice. It was enough to bring Jessica's head up. Marcelle never let emotion get involved in her job. Today she sounded troubled. Marcelle?

"Send them in, Marcelle, and then some fresh coffee, please."

"Right away, sir," the Yeoman said as she stepped back.

Senior Flight Centurion Milos Pavlovic, *Jouster*, stood in the doorway, an extremely anxious and ashen look on his face.

Oh, what the hell?

"Come in, *Jouster*. Sit. What can I do for you?"

She watched him move carefully, precisely, like he was at pains to do everything right. His field uniform even looked cleaned. *What was he up to now?*

"Sir," he said quietly as he sat, "I've come to apologize."

Jessica leaned back with an apprising look on her face. Not quite the last thing she expected to hear today, or from him, but very, very close.

"Really? Do tell." She couldn't keep the tartness out of her voice even if she wanted to, so she didn't try.

To his credit, he flinched at the tone and subsided instead of lashing out.

He took a deep breath, obviously working from a rehearsed speech about how he had learned from his mistakes and would be a better pilot and leader in the future.

She almost threw him out of her office right then, just on general principle, but something about his body language stayed his execution.

"Up until yesterday," he said, quietly, diffidently. It was so far out of character that she had to lean forward to hear him. "I thought I was a better tactical officer, a better battle manager, than you."

He paused and took another breath.

Jessica wiped all trace of emotion from her face and paid close attention.

"You called me a lazy amateur going through the motions, suggesting that you would have handled it entirely differently and your method would have succeeded completely, where I got deeper and deeper into trouble."

"I did," she said, just as quietly. She would have lost money betting with any number of people that she would never have heard even this much contrition out of *Jouster*. "Am I wrong?"

"No, damn it," he growled, more at himself than at her. "And that just makes it worse. I was flying on autopilot, doing exactly what the book says not to do, trusting that I was so much better than the other guy that I could get away with it. I got in over my head and had to be rescued."

He paused again. Took another labored breath.

"And I got one of my own killed. Gustav Papp wasn't my best pilot, or my best friend, or even my favorite wingmate, but he died saving my butt from my own stupidity. I killed *Ironside*."

"That you did, *Jouster*," Jessica said quietly into the gap. "Do you understand now why I don't trust you?"

He gave her a pained look, like this was the first time he had ever looked into his own soul. Knowing him, it might have been.

She let him stew.

"So then I talked to the First Officer, looking for sympathy," the man continued. "He told me to grow up."

"I see," Jessica said, mentally adding a gold star next to Jež's name. Her First Officer was turning into a proper commander. That alone would make everything else almost a bonus to her task.

"So I went down to the tactical simulator bay, all set to prove you wrong, Commander. To show that there was no better way to handle the situation."

Jessica noted that the pilot had developed a pitch of fire to his voice. It was like watching the stages of death play out before her eyes.

"I spent the next twelve hours studying you, looking for that signature move that you think would have worked at *C'Xindo*. I studied *Iger*, *St. Germaine*, *Hulun Buir*, and *Bratsk*."

"Interesting," she said. This conversation was already well beyond what she expected. "What did you find, *Jouster*?"

"You don't have a signature move," he said, almost angry at her, or, more likely, himself. "Every battle you won by using an entirely different maneuver, or trick, or sailing plan. There was no pattern to it."

"There's not supposed to be," she admitted. "Predictability equals death."

"I realize that," he cried, voice moving up half an octave, "but I had to find something, anything to prove you wrong. And it wasn't there."

He gasped and took a heavy breath, obviously working to calm himself.

Jessica was impressed. This was a side even his personnel files hadn't hinted at.

"So then I thought about you as a person," he continued.

Jessica had to fight a grin off of her face.

That might be the first time he had ever thought of her as a person rather than a commander, or a taskmaster, or a piece of ass he might chase.

She kept her face serious. He probably deserved better than her thoughts about him at this moment.

"What struck me as utterly unique about you was *Valse d'Glaive*. The Dance of Swords. So I spent four hours studying the art form, watching video. It is an unlikely combination of two ancient fighting forms from the Homeworld, from cultures a hemisphere apart. *Tai Chi*, which people still practice today, and Florentine-style fencing, from a city in a nation-state on a planet that was destroyed three thousand years ago."

"The Dance Of Swords?" she asked, intrigued by his line of thinking. He might be on to something that someone else could exploit.

"Aye, *Valse d'Glaive*," he replied. "A blade in each hand, able to attack or defend equally well and from either direction. But coupled with movement. Acrobatics, tumbles, leaps. Misdirection. So I went back to each of those battles, and I saw what you did."

"What did I do, *Jouster*?" she said quietly, intrigued for the first time.

"You let them commit, Commander. Forced them to commit, in fact, either to the obvious blow or the misdirection. It didn't matter to you which way they committed. Once they did, the other hand struck. Every time. Every single time."

Jessica felt a moment of *déjà vu* overwhelm her. She flashed back sixteen years to Nils Kasum saying almost the exact same words to her while grading her final in Advanced Tactics.

She leaned forward and studied the man in front of her, chin resting on a fist as her eyes bored in. Interesting. *So I might have to do something predictable soon, just to keep being unpredictable?*

"So how would you win at *C'Xindo, Jouster*?" She couldn't help sounding like Nils Kasum right now. It was like he was standing in the corner, watching. Hopefully applauding.

"Pick a pole," he said. "Probably the southern one since the squadron was planning to climb out of the ecliptic after their strafing pass."

"Go on," she smiled at him, much warmer than she would have thirty seconds ago.

"The BattleTug Captain has already committed to racing around the planet to try and get a shot at *Rajput* or *Auberon* as they go by. It won't be much of a shot, because we caught them so far out of position, but they're really, really trying. If I had gone under the pole, we might have been able to get underneath of him before he even noticed we were there. Tactical simulator suggests a worst case we could only have two missiles home as we blew by him at full speed. Best case, five of six. The difference is a month in drydock versus possibly enough damage to have killed her right there in orbit."

He paused and took a deep breath. He held it so long she thought he was done and was about to reply.

"Instead," the man continued, "I took the obvious path, a pursuit course right into orbit with him where the defense fighters could catch us. We did barely any damage at all, and I killed Flight Centurion Papp. You saw it intuitively and wouldn't have made that mistake."

All the air trailed out him like a balloon. He even seemed to sag in on himself.

Jessica was completely amazed. Utterly blown away. She had been expecting to transfer his sullen ass on to some next Commander to deal with.

"Two things, Senior Flight Centurion Pavlovic," she said calmly, firmly, trying to break through to him before the man simply gave up. "First, people die in war. Yours is the single most dangerous Occupation Specialty in the *RAN*. *Ironside* and little miss *Bitter Kitten* took on five enemy fighters, got three of them, and almost got away, but for a defense missile launched by the BattleTug as they flew by. He was, in fact, protecting her rear as she got all three kills."

"She did that?"

The incredulity in his voice was a wonder, but she needed to break through to him now, before she lost him completely.

"She did. Now, second point," she pressed home. "I saw the same maneuver you did, because I plotted out every possible scenario I could think of in the eighteen minutes while we jumped deeper in system. There was nothing intuitive about it."

"Nothing?"

"No, mister," she felt her own anger begin to boil, building on the energy that seemed to have flowed out of him. "At *Iger*? I'll let you in on a secret that only the First Lord knows. I had seventeen contingency maneuvers planned. *St. Germaine*? Six. *Hulun Buir*? Eleven. I could go on. The point is that I spend a great deal of time in the Tactical Simulators, plotting possible scenarios and how I would respond. Then I game them out to an end point, rewind to an interesting spot, and try a different outcome."

"Really?" he said, quiet again.

"I suggest, *Jouster*," she replied, "that you spend less time working on your gun skills and more on your command skills. Learn to think like the enemy and out-guess them. That will keep you alive."

"Yeah," he said glumly.

There was a long pause. She let him think.

"So I came here to apologize to you, Commander," he said finally. "I was angry, then embarrassed, and then confused. I let you down. I let my people down. I'm sorry."

For a long moment, Jessica was sure she could see his soul. He was that open. It was almost scary to be able to look so deep into someone. She couldn't imagine ever baring her soul, or her neck, so much, for anyone.

"Apology accepted, Senior Flight Centurion Milos Pavlovic," she whispered. The moment needed quiet. "Are you ready to fly again?"

"Sir?"

"I have one more test for you, *Jouster*," she said. "I was going to have *Uller* do it, but I'm willing to torture you with it instead."

"Aye, sir. Do your worst."

"You'll be tasked with flying close escort on *Auberon*. We'll have both of your launch rails loaded with *Shot* missiles. Useful for attacking other fighters and killing inbound missiles, but not much more than that."

She gestured to the ship around them. "I plan to fly this great gray beast right down their throats. They will ignore everyone else, *Rajput*, *CR-264*, the Flight Wing, so they can concentrate on *Auberon*. We will just be too big a target to pass up."

"They'll commit to you, and leave themselves wide open."

She could hear the wonderment in his voice as the image clicked in his mind.

"Correct," she said. "This time, *Necromancer* will be the live blade."

CHAPTER XXXIV

Date of the Republic April 8, 393 Ladaux

This was another committee hearing room, although smaller than the grand public one.

Nils had his scowl firmly pasted to his face by the time he followed the Premier into the chamber.

He looked forward to what was about to happen, but shouldn't look too gleeful. Much.

Tadej appeared angry enough to chew nails.

The Premier waited for the hubbub at their entrance to settle.

All sound died, even breathing. Eyes dropped as the Premier's gaze settled on faces.

"Those of you who were involved, and I will know all of those names by the end of the day, will stay," Tadej announced in a voice sharp enough to shave on. "Everyone else will depart immediately. This will be a private meeting."

A moment of confused silence passed.

"Move!" The Premier's voice, the former First Fleet Lord's voice, rattle the chandelier overhead.

A handful of Senators rose with the general mob of staff and happily made their way to the door, obviously relieved to have escaped with their careers, if not their dignity, somewhat intact.

The man who had been squatting behind the Chairman rose to leave as well, but was stopped by Tadej before he took a whole step. "Brant," Tadej thundered before dropping down to a normal speaking voice, "you will stay. You may, in fact, have a seat next to the Chairman. You will be sharing his fate."

Nils was impressed. The Chairman's aide shrugged, nodded politely, and settled quickly into a chair without a glance back at his boss.

In less than a minute, the room was down to six of the seventeen Senators, plus a handful of others, Senatorial staff who had decided that their fingerprints would be too obvious to scrub off.

The Premier walked to one end of the long table, forcing all heads to follow him. He put a hand down on the table as he leaned forward.

Nils was taken with the image of a headmaster about to lecture a mob of unruly middle school students. Probably not the most inaccurate description, all things considered.

Tadej let the moment hang far longer than the situation called for. From his face, he was not having a problem with the right word. Perhaps the right profanity to sum it all up in one word, if one existed, but that was something else.

"There exists," he said finally, conversationally, "a report, detailing an attack on the Imperial planet of *Ao-Shun*, in the system *2218 Svati Prime*, am I correct?"

Heads nodded enthusiastically.

Tadej nodded back at them once.

"And the report suggests that Command Centurion Jessica Keller aboard the vessel *RAN Auberon* attacked the planet with bio-weapons and radioactive isotopes, yes?"

More nods. Nils stood perfectly still by the front door and watched the Premier work. It was art.

This was why he let his brother handle the political side of things. The Aquitaine Navy was so much more pure and clean. Generally.

"She did not."

The Premier let the stunned silence stretch.

"I have only just now read the executive summary of her own report, on my way down here to prevent you from committing further treason to the

Republic," Tadej stressed the word *Republic*, but Nils could tell the operative word that got everyone's attention was still *Treason*.

Senators could be executed for treason. Four had been, although none in a century.

"So could someone point to the section of the report detailing Command Centurion Keller's Crimes Against Humanity and General Crimes under the Republic Code?" It sounded like such a polite request. Like asking someone where they wanted to have lunch.

It took a moment for the realization to sink in. Followed by the panic.

Heads turned towards three people. The Chairman, his aide Brant, and Senator Tomčič. Hanging was in the cards, from those looks.

The Chairman, Patriarch of one of the wealthiest shipping clans on *Anameleck Prime*, sputtered as he worked up the words. "She must have done something," he tried to thunder. It came out weak and indecisive. "Why else would she drop a bomb on the planet and kill people?"

Nils stepped forward at this point. *When better to kick an old enemy, than when he was down?*

"Premier," he said, "according to Keller's report, the device was aimed at the uninhabited north pole of the planet, and detonated at an altitude of approximately 73,000 meters above sea level. The nearest town of any size was approximately 8,000 linear kilometers away from the blast."

"Thank you, First Lord," Tadej said graciously. He turned to the rest of the room with a warm smile, and a velvet hammer. "So we have Keller's report. I have read that one in great detail, by the way, something none of you have done yet, I promise. That leads me to another interesting question. Where did your report originate?"

Even Nils was astounded at the mastery with which the Premier sprung his trap. And he was, oh so happy that he wasn't in that net.

The silence stretched awkwardly.

"*Wilankadu*," Tomčič finally spoke up.

"Ah," the Premier smiled. He reached out and opened a copy of the report in question and flipped through it until he found the page he desired. "I see. The Independent Cantons managed to complete a detailed investigation of *Ao-Shun* in just eighty days, despite not having any resources in the region. In fact, it appears that this report, in footnote 143, specifically requests that the *Independent Cantons of Wilankadu* conduct just such an investigation. And how, just how, did it arrive here to *Ladaux* so quickly? Anyone?"

He scowled furiously down the table at the uncomfortable faces.

One of the quieter Senators spoke up finally. It was hard to hear his voice. It would have been lost in any greater level of noise. "It was my understanding," he said, "that it was delivered to the Chairman by the Imperial Ambassador, under seal."

Tadej smiled at the group. "Is that so? And we immediately take the word of our sworn enemy and use it to try to destroy one of our own naval officers? Is that how the Senate works, these day?"

Nils watched him walk angrily down the front of the table now. He stopped exactly midway between the Chairman and Senator Tomčič and turned towards them.

"Because if that is the case, ladies and gentlemen," he continued, voice rising louder, "then I believe we could make a strong legal case for collaboration. The crime is Aiding and Abetting Enemies of the Republic. The *Fribourg Empire* is our enemy, although some of you seem to have forgotten that in your mad quest for revenge."

He slammed an open palm on the table for emphasis. "This will end, right here, right now. If you want a witch hunt, I will provide the press enough witches that the Senate needs to hold new elections in order to seat a quorum. Am I understood?"

Heads nodded. Nils found his own unconsciously among them. He kept his smile inside. There really was no doubt why this man was in charge.

Tadej pointed at the Chairman with a finger that looked like Zeus's bolt ready to fly. "You will print an apology to Keller and a retraction in the press. I don't care if it is buried on page six. I want it in print. Tomorrow."

Tadej turned to Nils with that same finger. "And you will make sure that that apology is delivered to her with the next supply run, so she is not spending her time worrying about fools on the home front when she should be fighting a war."

"Aye, sir," Nils nodded. "It will be done."

Tadej turned back to the rest of the room. "Here is the deal I will offer you. Keller is now under my protection, not just the First Lord's. If you decide to go after her, I will forward this entire affair to the Grand Justice Of the Republic and ask her to investigate everyone in this room, absolutely everyone involved, for treason. Senatorial immunity will be revoked for the course of such an investigation."

Even Nils hung on his words. Short of an actual execution, this was about as dangerous as politics in the *Republic* ever got.

The silence became oppressive. "I see we have an understanding, then, ladies and gentlemen. Please convey it to all the key players not in this room as well. I am not happy. I am not bluffing."

He turned his back on the Senators at that point and deliberately smiled at Nils as he began walking towards the door.

"First Lord," he said, "I would greatly appreciate if you would join me for dinner. We will need to see how we can salvage the *Cahllepp Frontier* from all this amateur meddling."

They exited the room, arm in arm.

Nils looked at the bottom of the bottle owlishly. That was the fourth? Fifth?

It had been very good wine, wrapped around an amazingly good meal. He looked across the private booth to his old schoolmate chum, Tadej, equally owlish.

The man burped.

"We're going to have to publish at least some of Project Mischief in the press soon," the Premier muttered darkly. "Otherwise, too many people will be calling for her head on a pike."

"Not all," the First Lord replied evasively. "Just the bits about how the bomb was constructed. Some of the other ideas need time to be used on the *Fribourgers*."

"So, Nils," he began, "what will you do with Keller?"

"Well, Tad," Nils hiccupped, "I had hoped to leave her out there for a year under an independent command and let her cover herself and her crew in such glory that we had to promote her to Fleet Lord and bring her back to the main action. Not sure what to do now."

Tadej nodded sagely and looked at the shattered remains of his tiramisu. "I think it might be wiser to leave her there for a while, Nils. If she's causing this much grief to the *Fribourgers* in the first six months, imagine what she could do with time and support."

"Well, yes," Nils said, "but I don't want her forgotten out there. I've read the dossiers on her officers and many of them should never have been sent that far from the main fleets. Something is wrong in my own organization to allow it."

"Well, you do your job and sort it out," the Premier said quietly, "I have long term plans for that woman."

Nils couldn't help the shudder than ran down his spine at the Premier's words.

What plans?

CHAPTER XXXV

Date of the Republic March 17, 393 Top of the 2218 Svati Prime system

It was seductive, watching the big projection slowly rotate above the table. Jessica sat in her big, comfortable Flag Bridge chair and contemplated the possibilities it offered her.

All the usual faces were ghosts around the edge of her command table, comfortable in their own chairs on their own bridges.

"So, people," she began, "normally we drop out of Jumpspace fairly close, and then hit them quickly. Today, we landed as far out as we could scan, and clear at the top of the system, rather than below or on the ecliptic. I was reminded recently of the need to be unpredictable." She smiled at what *Jouster* had done for her, even accidentally.

It felt strange, both owing that man good favor, and smiling all by itself.

"I wanted time to see what we were getting ourselves into, since they've already seen us once."

She paused to sip her coffee. Others hit their own mugs.

"Giroux, you've had thirty minutes to listen to signals traffic. What do we know?"

She was caught by surprise when the man actually looked up from his panels and gauges and made solid eye contact with her projection. He did it so rarely. He dialed up the scale of the projection.

"Sir, you really need to see this," he said, centering the image on a blue dot orbiting *Ao-Shun* closely.

Jessica read the transponder display next to the signal, twice.

"Confirmed?" she said softly.

"Aye, sir," Giroux smiled at her. "She is the *St. Albertus Magnus*, a hospital and research ship from the *Independent Cantons of Wilankadu*."

They shared the smile for a moment until the others began to grow restless.

"So," Jessica said, "they've brought in a medical research ship to uncover what we've done. People, we've just doubled the cost the Empire is paying to maintain their forces along this frontier, although the ship itself represents a problem."

"No, sir, an opportunity," the Flag Centurion spoke up suddenly from across the table. He was practically vibrating with energy.

"Go on, Enej."

"Aye, sir," the young man said. "The ship in question flies mercy missions for plagues, disasters, that sort of thing, right? Usually under private and very expensive contract to whoever needs them to come in, sometimes as a charity. It is still a very expensive ship to operate."

"Correct, Centurion," d'Maine said from the bridge of *Rajput*. His scowl might have been used to polish granite. "She is also a neutral vessel. Anything we do to her will reflect very poorly on us at our later court martials. You blow her up and you might as well hang yourself and save the Admiralty the trouble, lad."

"Yes," Enej agreed, "but she happens to be working in an active war zone, probably under contract right now, directly for the Emperor. That means she's not a neutral. We could capture her under the formal Rules Of War and ransom her back to *Wilankadu* later, maybe for a single *Lev*, maybe for the value of her hull. And maybe, just maybe, for a pirate's ransom."

Jessica watched the shark smiles grow around her. Her people were finally beginning to think like pirates.

"Enej, it sounds like you have some ideas for how to handle it. We'll talk off-line, but you'll be in charge of capturing *St. Albertus Magnus* while the rest of us go to work on the defenders."

Jež cleared his throat at that. "Sir, are you sure it is a wise idea to adopt this particular formation?"

"Meaning, am I insane for putting *Auberon* on point, the whole Flight Wing on one flank, and *Rajput* and *CR-264* on the other?"

"Your words, sir," Denis agreed with her, "but essentially yes. Are you nuts?"

She smiled. Six months ago, he would have simply nodded and figured out how to execute her orders. Now he was trying to anticipate her and have his own contingencies in place.

She could leave the ship to him and command just the squadron for the first time.

It felt good.

She took a moment to let her smile encompass all of them. "*Auberon* was built on a Heavy Cruiser hull, people. We don't have all the firepower of a Heavy Cruiser, but they don't have anything over there heavy enough to fight us toe-to-toe. If they divide three ways to engage us, we annihilate them. Not just defeat them. Annihilate them."

She took another sip of coffee and let that sink in.

They were a main-line combat squadron, keyed up and trained, taking on country militias, with surprise on their side. As long as the odds stayed in their favor, they just had to be careful and hit with sledgehammers instead of snowballs. Most of the time.

Ao-Shun had required a snowball the first time. What was coming next would be even worse. Meaner at least. Something like kicking puppies.

"So I expect them to have to decide who to go after, an up-gunned Flight Wing with a Gunship in the middle, a Heavy Destroyer with a Fleet Escort riding shotgun, or a Strike Carrier."

"They'll go for you," d'Maine said, "biggest and most important ship. Best return on their investment."

Jessica smiled. "I'm counting on it."

CHAPTER XXXVI

Date of the Republic March 17, 393 2218 Svati Prime system

The launch tube was a dark, forbidding place. It felt cold, but that was purely psychological.

Jouster sat in his cockpit and listened to the comm traffic. *Southbound* had taken command in his absence, and was doing a competent job. Far less flashy than he would have done. *But wasn't that the point? He would sit here and do his job and convince the Dragon Lady on the bridge that he was fit to fly. Growing up sucked, but sometimes it had to be done.*

Everything out there looked pretty on the scanner.

The four M-5 *Harpoon* fighters rode escort for the two Saturation bombers, *Damocles* and *Starfall*, with the big Gunship, *Necromancer* holding station just below them. *da Vinci* rode above and behind, like the stinger on a scorpion.

It was a formation he had originated and perfected.

And he wasn't there with them. There was nothing else to do but watch them on the scanner and let them do the fighting.

Now he understood how *da Vinci* felt. All Ainsley had to do in battle was watch the screen and keep the bad guys from sneaking up on them. *When was the last time she had actually fired her guns?*

Below, it was just like the tactical simulator had predicted. The station they had gutted last time was repaired and operational again, probably at a stupidly great cost.

The pilots over there were much faster off the block than last time, as well. And, instead of the normal twelve fighters that made up an Imperial squadron, he watched sixteen signals emerge from the station.

Nobody seemed to be paying attention. And she hadn't ordered him to be silent. Maybe it was time to act like a Flight Leader.

"*da Vinci*, this is *Jouster*," he said, trying to maintain a bored tone to his voice for everyone else listening. He felt like he was being graded by the Dragon Lady every time he spoke. He probably was.

"Go ahead, *Jouster*," she said after a moment, probably of surprise.

"*da Vinci*, take a really hard look at those last four signals, the group that is at the back of the diamond formation. Imperials don't break squadrons of fighters up, ever. Live together, train together, fight together." He took a breath, fighting the urge to look backwards over his shoulder to see if Keller was standing there. "I'm guessing they brought something heavier to the dance and don't want us to realize it until they get close."

"Roger that, *Jouster*," she said. "Stand by."

Jouster let out a breath. Nobody had said anything sarcastic or rude.

"Squadron, this is *da Vinci*," Ainsley announced over the general push. "Credit *Jouster* with the catch. Enemy fighters consist of a standard squadron of A-7b fighters, escorting a quad of A-3f strike fighters. Expect a lot of missiles in your immediate future. All craft, make sure your counter-measures are armed."

"*da Vinci*, this is *Auberon*," he heard *her* voice over the comm. Keller really had gotten into his head. He flinched, waiting for the next words. "Acknowledged. Good eyes, *Jouster*. Thank you."

Wow. Really? Credit? But I'm just sitting here in the forward launch bay, twiddling my thumbs.

Another voice sounded in his head. The woman who had been his original flight instructor, once upon a time. Back when he was a punk. A bigger punk.

Yeah, Pavlovic, she said, *but instead of sulking, you found something useful to do. Something that will keep your teammates alive.*

Oh.

He went back to the scanner and rotated it 150 degrees to see what things looked like to someone standing on the surface of the planet. *What else could he find?*

Jessica nodded. Wachturm had justified her paranoia, once again.

That man, that Admiral, that tactical genius was damned good. Mixing up fighters and strike craft, and having them all act alike until they got on top of someone, that was a recipe for disaster for her. But only if she was unprepared.

Hopefully this would work.

She watched the projection in the big tank. *Rajput* and *CR-264* coming in softly on the right flank. Out front, but not far out front. Enough to make you pick your poison. The whole Flight Wing, minus *Jouster*, flying hard and aggressive on the left flank.

Right now, her fear was that the defenders would go after the ships on her right. If they went at the fighters, it would be roughly even for firepower, plus all the surprises she could bring to bear with *Auberon*. But that many defenders could swarm *Rajput* and *CR-264* and do crippling damage before the two ships could be extricated.

"Flag Centurion," she said, "status on the Imperial squadron?"

She waited as he continued to study his screen. "So far, sir, they are still tracking on us. Sixty second to the point of no return."

"Anybody else threatening us?" she asked, mentally counting down the seconds.

"Negative, per the Science Officer," came the reply. "Giroux says the station is being very quiet. Most of the traffic in the system is staying put instead of trying to run from us, this time."

"That's good," Jessica observed. "They learned to stay close on the expectation that we aren't staying around. We should do something about that."

"Sir?"

"Next time, Enej. We'll stay on plan today."

"Roger that. Imperial fighters have passed the way point. If they try to turn now, they'll miss everything."

"Roger that, Enej. Tell Jež to alert *Jouster* and Tamara. I expect all hell to break loose shortly."

"They confirm ready status already, commander," he said.

"Ahead of me?"

"On plan, sir."

"Good." She turned and looked over her shoulder. "Marcelle, could you bring me some fresh coffee, please. They seem to have thing under control here."

"Aye, sir," The woman unbuckled and rose with a smirk on her face. At least some things never changed.

It was nice not having to share Marcelle with the rest of the crew.

Jessica watched the projection for perhaps ten seconds when the center flashed bright and lights in the room turned red. A mournful horn played softly in the background, in case anybody was not paying attention.

Time for war.

She watched Jež's face on the projection, even though he wasn't paying attention to her.

"Flight Deck," he said firmly. "Enemy squadron has fired everything they have at us. Crash launch *Jouster*. Break. All guns except primaries to defensive fire until otherwise ordered. Tactical Officer has command. Damage control parties stand by."

Jouster always got a rush from the acceleration pushing him back into his seat. The launch rails literally flung you clear of the ship like an arrow, away and slightly down to clear the bow of the ship in case you had to maneuver. Normally, he redlined things from there, the faster to get to the bad guys.

Today, he held his throttle medium, left the yoke centered, and focused on his scan board. He felt like a small dog on a short leash. Probably looked like one, too.

They had launched missiles earlier than he had expected, but almost to the second when Keller's simulation had predicted. It was kind of eerie.

The wall of missiles coming at him was absolutely frightening to consider.

Someone over there was just plain paranoid. Twelve melee fighters, each firing two missiles. Except two had failed, so twenty-two missiles inbound. Plus four strike fighters that had each fired six more as fast as they could separate. And each of those had launched cleanly, so twenty-four more.

Jouster considered forty-six missiles incoming and did the math in his head. That was enough firepower to blow a couple of Republic dreadnaughts into space kibble, let alone one Strike Carrier. He sure hoped she knew what she was doing. This was cutting it awful damned close.

His targeting computer beeped. Not like it needed much of a firing solution for what was about to happen, but it was still nice that the locks were solid.

He thumbed the launch button and felt his craft shudder under the jolt as both missiles jumped away from him.

As he watched his scanners, the two missiles each opened like flowers, shedding their warhead casings to reveal internal arrays of micro-missiles. He hated the *Shot* missiles. Any single one of those sub-missiles was enough to cripple a fighter like his in melee and they were a pain to kill. They were, however, medicine for what evil ailed him today.

His scanner threatened to overload as his two missile tracks turned into eight. Overhead, *Auberon* had launched two more of the sub-munition killer missiles.

Sixteen going out. Forty-six coming in. It still didn't seem fair.

Two bright flashes of light, followed by two lesser bolts as *Auberon* opened up at long range with the big Type-3 Secondaries and then the Type-2's. Those were for engaging other warships, not missiles, although the Type-2 was a lovely thing to kill fighter craft with.

Other fighters.

At the right edge of his screen, he saw *Rajput* start to speak as well. Four of her missiles inbound suddenly turned into sixteen warheads as she brought her forward wing batteries to bear at extreme long distance. From his left, the two S-11 *Orcas* spoke as well.

Holy cow, was that every single Shot missile in the squadron? It must be, these guys only launched eight combined, and those two battle sleds held nine launch rails each. So they must still have something for the dance.

Jouster watched the wall of miniature missiles converging with something like awe. He remembered to close his mouth. Twice.

Thirty-two friendly signals from the left. Sixteen from the right. Sixteen in front of him.

Wow.

It was a vision of hell. There was no other way to describe it.

It was even bigger than the time he had been part of the Wing that got in the kill shot on the old Imperial Battleship *Klagenfurt*. She had gone up like a supernova.

This burst of light was so bright it hurt his eyes, even from this distance.

As his eyes cleared, an alarm sounded on his console. One of the Imperial missiles had gotten through all that mess intact.

Impact in four seconds. Right on Auberon's nose.

Jouster punched the throttle to the top and brought his thumb to the firing stud.

Chances of shooting an incoming missile at this speed?
None.
Do it anyway.
He pulled back the yoke and centered himself on the missiles flight path.
Chances of it hitting me on this path, or mistaking me for Auberon?
Pretty good.
And I owe her for the chance to go out fighting.
Jouster held the firing stud down and watched his guns cycle.

He imagined he could see the onrushing missile, a gray bullet with Imperial flags down both sides, but at the approaching speed, that was unlikely.

He took a deep breath.

Impact in one.

Nothing.

A flash of light in front of him, turning into a ball of fire he was about to fly through. Flew through. His whole fighter craft rattled.

What the hell?

"*Jouster,* this is *Auberon,*" he still heard Keller's voice. He must be in hell now. "What is your status?"

Status?

Jouster realized he wasn't dead.

His shields were degraded almost to tissue paper as he barrel-rolled away from the heat and into the clear. They would be minutes recovering.

"*Auberon,* all systems nominal," he replied, lizard-brain training, at least, still working.

Up ahead, the sixteen assholes who had just fired a shit-storm of missiles at him. He was feeling uncharitable. Too bad they were too far away for his Type-1's to do anything.

"Roger that, *Jouster,*" he heard the Commander say. "Nice flying and thank you. You'll owe Nina Vanek and Moirrey Kermode drinks after this."

"What happened, *Auberon?*" He was sure he was supposed to be dead right now. *Was this what hell looked like?*

"Those two put an ace in the hole where the secondary observatory used to be. We still have exactly one of those missiles left, until we get back to base. Now, are you ready to tango, *Jouster?*"

"Any time, *Auberon,*" he said. Apparently, she didn't hold a grudge as long as he feared.

"Break. Squadron, this is the Flag." Her voice took on a new timbre. Hard. Ruthless. It had sounded mean before. Now it sounded like the Voice of Doom. He was glad she was finally mad at someone else. "Engage the enemy squadron with everything you have. *Jouster*, you are cleared from escort duties. Proceed to melee."

"Roger that, *Auberon*." Over there, there were a few people who owed him. Running from his Flight Wing was not going to save them long.

CHAPTER XXXVII

Date of the Republic March 17, 393 2218 Svati Prime system

Jessica watched the beginning of the dogfight long enough to assume the conclusion. First, the Imperials had launched everything they had in their desperate gamble to kill *Auberon*. Thank the Creator the planners over there were at least a little predictable. That trick would have simply vaporized *Rajput*.

Then, they discovered that they were about to be caught in a pincer as the two wings suddenly pivoted in and began to converge, with both *Auberon* and *Rajput* opening fire with the big Type-3's from the edge of touch.

Hits with the big Secondaries were rare at this range, but a fighter just evaporated when they did. Two had already found that out the hard way before the rest turned and tried to flee, right across the bows of the Flight Wing, suddenly crossing their T from the left.

Enej Zivkovic got her attention more with the tone of his voice and his body language than anything. Not that he had any butt to speak of to get her attention, otherwise.

Her Flag Centurion was facing away from her, so she could watch his back and shoulders as he ranted into a sound-deadening microphone.

Today, he moved like a predator, a big cat stalking the last few steps. No, strike that, a small cat who just nabbed himself a canary.

She watched him key a line to Jež and lean back down into his seat with a contented air as he glanced over at her.

"Bridge, this is the Flag," he said, suddenly realizing as he spoke that he had an audience. He sat up straighter in his chair and actually blushed.

"Go ahead," the First Officer said from his station. It was much noisier at the far end.

"Jež, please clear *Cayenne* to launch soonest with a full deployment of marines. *St. Albertus Magnus* has struck her colors and is ransoming the crew and vessel on good behavior until we arrive to take possession. Oh, and you should send along a navigator. I don't trust theirs. Cheers."

She watched Enej close the channel and smile at her. She recognized the smile. She had seen it on others recently.

"What did you do, Enej?" she asked quietly across the space.

"I told them, Commander," he said as he pulled his jacket more properly straight, "that if they didn't strike immediately, we would do the same thing to them we did to *Ao-Shun*."

"Which was psychological warfare masquerading as mind games that amounted to exactly nothing."

"Hey," he said, affronted, "I'm not going to tell them that. Besides, technically, we did. Or we're about to."

She couldn't stop the snort of laughter that escaped her mouth, although she did wipe it physically off and paste her command scowl more properly in place.

"They do have a Legal Affairs Officer over there, Enej," she replied after a breath. "One whose job it is to argue those sorts of things."

"I will happily stand in an Aquitaine Naval Court and make my case, once we tell them the truth."

"You probably will, Centurion." She watched him blink in surprise. A crestfallen look crept across his features. "However, you are in the right, so you'll be safe."

He took a breath and turned hastily back to his board.

"What else do we have, Enej," she said.

"Not much, sir," he replied, scanning his boards. "Two of the Imperial fighters managed to escape the Closing of the Red Sea, but they did so by redlining their engines and pretty much burning them out. One should make orbit with enough power to maneuver. The other one looks like he might miss the planet completely and drift into deep space."

Jessica considered the slaughter she had already unleashed, plus what was coming. There was enough blood for one day.

"Keep a watch on both. Have *Cayenne* act as a rescue tug if they send out a distress call. And have *Gaucho* carrying a medical crew with him, as well as his boarding parties. They might be injured and they will most certainly be prisoners."

"Aye, sir."

Jessica watched the dogfight fade down into a pair of brief flashes of light. All of the green lights were still there. None of the gold ones were left. She checked the status and noted the damage. *Bitter Kitten* had three more kills, and apparently was holding her little fighter together purely by force of will, if the damage report was to believed. Everyone else had some level of mauling, but nothing critical.

"Time to Phase 3, Enej?" she asked sharply, not looking up from her projection. *Cayenne* might need to rescue Lagunov before they did anything else.

"Seventy-three minutes, commander." The reply was just as tight. He was looking at the same data.

"Recall the fighter wing right now. *da Vinci* and the *Orcas* can escort *Necromancer* into position from here. I'll notify Iskra."

"On it."

She pushed a button and sent her voice to the whole ship. Most of the crew would have some method of following the battle, but it didn't have any commentary explaining why things were happening. That was reserved for her and the bridge crew.

"Flight Deck, this is the Flag," she said calmly. Calm officer transmit their calmness to their crews. So did nervous ones. "Recalling *Southbound* and hers. Stand by for possible heavy landings."

As always, Iskra Vlahovic's message was a scrolling marquee reply. She almost never actually spoke into a comm unless forced to.

Damage Control parties already standing by. Thanks. Iskra

Jessica nodded. One less thing to worry about, if Lagunov could limp home.

She watched the planet swell slowly in her projection as *Auberon* drew closer.

"Giroux," she said over the comm, "has that station done anything at all since we arrived?"

She sipped her coffee and waited as her sensors officer went backwards through his logs.

"Negative, sir," came the reply. "After the fighters flew, she'd done nothing. No missiles, no Secondaries."

Jessica considered her options. There was a possibility they were playing possum over there. There was also a chance that they had scrimped on fixing everything else so they could get the fighter squadron in place and maybe were out of missiles right now and hoping nobody noticed.

She keyed open a relay to Alber' d'Maine. "*Rajput*, this is *Auberon*, what is your inventory on Primaries?"

She waited, expecting a delay while the counted. There was none.

"Full load, *Auberon*, minus one round discharged saluting the flag when we departed *Kismayo* last time out."

She nodded.

d'Maine was an old school Command Centurion. A superstitious lot who had been taught to always fire one weapon at the beginning of a voyage to prove that they still worked, and always keep that reload empty as a sop to Lady Luck.

She would have filled his rack on the last run home, but it wouldn't have done any good. He would have just fired it off again a day later.

Auberon was fully loaded. She didn't believe in letting Lady Luck have any advantage.

She keyed the squadron-wide comm open. *Let's let everyone hear this.*

"Squadron, this is the Flag," she announced firmly. "Order the inhabitants of the Imperial Station to abandon ship immediately. *Auberon* and *Rajput* will pass into Primary range of the station in exactly twenty-two minutes, and remain in range for roughly eight minutes after that. You will engage the station with Primaries at that time and maintain fire until she is destroyed or we pass out of range. If she is still intact at that time, we will make another pass later to finish the job. Do not fire on any civilian vessels unless fired upon first."

Jessica took a deep breath. War was hell, but there were no points for second place. She closed the general push and spoke across the space between them.

"Enej," she said quietly. "Transmit that audio to the station and all vessels in orbit on as many channels as you think necessary. Put it on a loop as well."

He looked at her with shock that slowly melted down to a grim nod as he went to work.

Nobody in his right mind would stay put over there now, knowing that they were about to be on the sharp end of something that took a Type-3 and jumped it up an order of magnitude.

That was how the Primary beam had been discovered in the first place. Someone had accidentally overloaded a Type-3 and blew it up, but not before it drilled a hole a goodly distance into the mantle of a nearby moon.

After that, they made them into weapons that fired like old-style cartridges. Insert a generator, overload it, toss the empty container aside to be melted down or reloaded back at base.

The people over there would have time to get out. Anybody left at that point was too stubborn to live anyway. And the civilian ships in orbit should feel safe enough to pick up survivors before those people had to test free-fall suits from orbit.

That was a good way to puke yourself empty.

After all, a barely-shielded station like that one would resist the Primaries about as well as a can of beans resisting a hammer.

Now, it was on to Phase 3.

CHAPTER XXXVIII

She would have liked to have been up on the bridge with Jež and the rest, but she needed the much-better communication facilities down here on the Flag Bridge, so Jessica watched the scene unfold from her comfortable chair.

As usual, her command staff was present virtually, with Enej being one of the few people seated around the conference room table. In addition, three new faces were on-line. Anastazja Slusarczyk, commander of *Necromancer*, watched from one side while her pilot maneuvered the GunShip into position.

On the projection of the system, it was like a bit of oil had been dropped onto a bowl of water. Other ships skittered away like bugs as the gunship approached.

Seated next to Jessica, Moirrey had been invited to join the group for this session. She was the most instrumental in what was about to happen.

The evil engineering gnome didn't look the least bit cowed to be in such company, even though she kept mostly to herself. According to her personnel file, she did that anyway.

The final screen was Jessica's Dragoon, Senior Centurion Phillip Navin Crncevic, commonly called *Navin the Black* by the crew, as if he were some ancient Viking come to life.

She hadn't had much interaction with the man. He tended to stay down in the training and arms bays and work with his people, but she could see the reason for his nickname.

He was at least two meters tall, and felt like two of her wide at the shoulders, with big hands that looked like they should be holding a boarding axe right now instead of a clipboard. His skin was ebony black and the shaved skull made him look extra-fierce, although the barely-there van dyke showed itself to be all gray with age and maturity.

Probably a figure from nightmares for some of the civilian medical workers and contractors on the hospital ship.

Or he would be going forward.

"Crncevic," Jessica said once everyone was organized, "any problems over there?"

She watched the man's image shrug at the camera. It looked like a minor earthquake moving a small mountain.

"I would have said my daughter could have handled this lot," he said with a voice that matched the frame, Biblical in depth and tone, "but she's all grown up now and serving as a marine Cornet on *Athena*. Maybe my wife."

"Is that the same wife who's a retired drill instructor, Navin?" Jež chimed in with a tease.

The big man smiled. "There's always that."

"Maybe we should have sent your son, you old viking," Tamara said. "The doctors over there probably would have appreciated having a librarian instead of a Norseman, anyway."

Jessica held her command scowl in place as the Dragoon looked down at himself and back up at the camera. "Do I look Finnish?" She really wanted to giggle.

Jessica had been to *Ballard* once, on an early deployment, transporting a group of medical researchers to the ancient university there, the Earth-born AI system that was Alexandria Station. The population of *Ballard* primarily was Finnish, but the planet had maintained a long and close trade relationship with one of the other Founders of modern civilization, *Zanzibar*, even after both worlds were absorbed into the *Republic of Aquitaine*.

Navin the Black would have fit right in on the streets of Ithome. She would have to tell him that, sometime.

"Enough, people," Jessica said instead. "*Necromancer*, Anastazja, what is your status?"

The woman had a no-nonsense air about her in everything she did, a quiet professional who stood in sharp contrast to *Cayenne's* commander, Hollis Dyson aka *Gaucho*.

Anastazja nodded at the screen as a placeholder while she looked down to check something on a panel in front of her. "In position, *Auberon*," she said, "ready whenever you give the word."

Jessica looked at each face around the table.

Expectancy greeted her. Smiles, even. The kind from people who had just survived doom. They had become a team. She would be able to do a great deal of damage to the Empire with a team like this.

Jessica pushed a button to send the audio channel to the whole squadron, encrypted at the highest level. Everyone wanted to hear what was coming next.

Moirrey was turning into a radio star.

"*Necromancer*, this is the Flag," she said, "you may fire when ready."

Anastazja looked down and pushed a button.

Jessica nodded at her evil engineering gnome with a smile and let the woman take over narration of *Ao-Shun's* doom again.

On the projection, they all watched four bolts of lightning spring out from *Necromancer* and fall into orbit around *Ao-Shun's* equator.

"Ooh," Moirrey began, falling into her lilt, "what's this? Mean, nasty *Auberon's* come back for more trouble? Haven't ye bastards done enough already, with the plagues and nightmares and blowin' t'ings all ta hell? Oh, crap, shooting stars now? Headed south from the pole? Not like last time. That one jes blew itself up and poisoned the whole damned planet."

A long minute passed as the four missiles fell into formation, a perfect square girdling the planet.

They held their formation for a ten seconds and then began broadcasting static as loud as they could on all channels, with the anthem of the *Republic of Aquitaine* playing very softly underneath it.

That was an extra special touch.

"Uh oh," Moirrey continued, "something just knocked out me afternoon soaps, and the game. Haven't they left yet? What do they want with us? Hey, is that music? Weird."

On the screen, the four probes brightened slightly as they moved forward with their choreography. From a porthole, Jessica knew she would be able to actually see at least two of them as they began to burn giant magnesium bars, each a wrist thick and three meters long.

From the ground, everyone should be able to see at least one new star in the sky, daytime or night.

"What's this then? Have we gots a new supernova next door? That thing's almost as bright as the sun. What hae those Republic bastards done naow? Ohmygod, they've come to finish us off fer good this time. AAAUUUGGGGHHHHH!!!! Somebody does something, please. Call the fire department. Call the police. Call the navy. Can't anybody do nothing about this?"

On the screen, the four lights flickered out as the probes burned themselves out and dove into the atmosphere to burn up.

Moirrey's voice dropped to almost nothing.

"And then, darkness fall across the land. The Evil Witch of the North cast her great and deadly spell upon *Ao-shun* and turned all the wee little people into newts. Can't anyone find a handsome prince to come save them? Or a beautiful princess to give 'ems a kiss and break the spell? All was woe as she turned her army and rode off into the ascending darkness."

Jessica just shook her head as she listened to the barely-suppressed giggles around the table.

"We now return yous to your regularly scheduled war," Moirrey concluded. "Please join us next week for more adventures of Denis the Hedgehog, In The Land Of the Giant People."

Jessica turned to her First Officer with an eyebrow. One translation of Jež was *hedgehog*.

He grinned back and her and shrugged.

So, an inside joke for the family. Another thing that would keep them going.

"Squadron, this is the Flag," she said crisply, "proceed to rendezvous at point *Omicron* and prepare for transition to Jumpspace."

It was almost time to go home and see what waited her. *Ao-Shun* was likely to rattle an awful lot of cages.

CHAPTER XXXIX

Date of the Republic March 23, 393 Qui-Ping system

She expected a lot of yelling shortly. What was unclear was who would be doing it.

Jessica sat in the big conference room down in Engineering for this meeting. She hadn't really needed the physical space for what was coming, but for the emotional volume it would be better.

Upstairs, the small conference room had a much more militaristic, judicial feel to it. That's why it was used for those sorts of things.

This conference room was where her evil engineering gnomes did their work. Probably while giggling and singing songs. They were that weird.

The door opened and Senior Centurion Denis Jež entered, dressed in his best field uniform, but not his formal dress attire. This was not a Court, nor was it a reception for visiting dignitaries. At least, not friendly ones. Not yet, anyway. The day was young.

The woman following Jež was extremely tall, taller even than he was. She was long and lanky, but moved with the smooth confidence of a ballerina.

Dr. Yuda Alyona.

She would have been Russian, once upon a time, back when it still existed as a place instead of a frame of mind. Ash-blond hair French-braided and down nearly to her waist. Bright eyes, sharp, somewhere between blue and green, depending on her mood. Her mind was just as sharp, with advanced degrees in medicine, chemistry, and several other things.

Dr. Alyona scowled at the room as she entered, locking eyes with Jessica even as she made her way to her seat at the head of the table, rather than across from Jessica.

Jessica guessed that the doctor wanted communication today, not confrontation.

Denis sat across from Jessica, next to *Auberon's* Surgeon, Dr. Zephan Samara, a fussy little man who had to be pried out of his Medical Bays to be here today, and only consenting to come when she informed him who their guest was.

Apparently, Dr. Alyona was his idol.

She was probably that for a number of people, considering her life and her work. She had even impressed a newly-minted officer on her very first cruise after Academy, twelve years ago, while being given a ride by the *RAN* to a field visit at Ballard.

Not that she was likely to remember Jessica.

Dr. Alyona sat primly, calmly, quietly. She suffered to be waited on. Tea, hot and black, with a dash of honey.

She fixed her gaze on Jessica. Studied her. Weighed her soul.

"So," she said finally, "the bright-eyed young Cornet has grown up to be a common pirate?"

Yes, she still had that razor-sharp tongue to go with the razor-sharp mind.

Jessica smiled to herself as she took a sip of coffee. It would be easy to get into an argument with this woman.

It would also serve no purpose.

She hadn't brought her Purser, *Auberon's* Legal Affairs Officer, to this meeting. That would just look like she was trying to hide behind legalisms. She had not brought her Flag Centurion, who really should have been here, simply because he would be a knot of contention with Dr. Alyona over the whole affair.

"It's good to see you again, as well, Dr. Alyona," Jessica replied politely.

"The Imperial Authorities at *Ao-Shun* are demanding that you be arrested and extradited to *St. Legier* to stand trial for a whole range of crimes, including, but not limited to Biological Warfare and Crimes Against Humanity."

"I'm aware of that," Jessica nodded.

Out of the corner of her eyes, she watched the impact of the conversation on Jež and Dr. Samara. Both seemed relaxed.

"However," Dr. Alyona continued, "Admiral Emmerich Wachturm, who is, I might add, a cousin of the Emperor, was not so sure. He said it didn't fit your personality."

Really, the Admiral had made enough of a study of her to say something like that to a civilian?

Jessica wasn't sure whether she should be honored or paranoid that she rated such attention. But, it was attention well wasted on this frontier.

If he was that focused on her, he would not be lending his tactical and strategic genius to the War Frontiers. On balance, it helped the *Republic*. That was no small thing, considering her mission.

"I'm surprised that I rate that highly in his eyes, Dr. Alyona, or yours. Especially if I am, to use your words, a common pirate."

The woman leaned forward and redoubled her intensity.

Jessica felt the impact of that personality concentrated on her. It was almost physical in its visceral tones.

"What did you do, Keller?" she bit off each word angrily as it came out, like bitter lemons, or nails driven into her flesh.

Jessica smiled enigmatically and let the moment hang.

"I am not at liberty to discuss that with you right now, Dr. Alyona," she said simply. "What you don't know won't hurt you. Your ignorance, in fact, lets me ransom you with a minimum of fuss. If you did know, you might have to be held as a prisoner of war for a very long time. I would like to avoid that, if possible."

The tall woman leaned back in her chair. A canny look, came over her face. "So why am I here, then?" she asked quietly. The anger had been for show, apparently, or was, more likely, just masked for now.

Jessica opened a folder on the table in front of her. "I had to check," she began, "because I simply could not remember. The medical community that is the hospital ship, *St. Albertus Magnus,* actually dates back to before the founding of the Republic by over seventy-five years."

Dr. Alyona looked confused now. Probably a safer way to get her off track.

"That's right, she said warily, "I plan to retire completely from public service during the quincentennial celebrations. What does that have to do with you?"

"I would like," Jessica continued, "to ask for your oath and your assistance."

"Would you?" The look she gave Jessica might wilt flowers. At least, the soft, weak kind. Not the ones with thorns that grew in aggressive brambles and crowded out the lesser vegetation.

Jessica's kind.

"I would."

"Why?"

Jessica smiled. It was a smile First Lord Kasum had taught her, long ago, in an Advanced Tactics class. It was not warm. It was not friendly. It offered no solace to the weary. Cats often offered it to voles.

"Because your ship was captured in an active war zone providing assistance to enemies of the *Republic of Aquitaine*. You struck you colors honorably, and have served your ransom with honor and dignity."

The doctor smiled slyly at her words.

"Your ship is another story."

Jessica watched the Doctor's face drop. That was what pure shock looked like.

"I could order all of your data banks wiped clean and upload just enough navigational data for you to get home in less than a year."

"You wouldn't dare," the woman hissed. She leaned forward like a gladiator flexing.

Jessica leaned forward as well, mirroring her.

The two men sat perfectly still rather than draw any attention to themselves. The room was electric with tension.

"It would certainly be the end of my career if I did so, Dr. Alyona. We both know how highly you and your staff are esteemed by both *Republic* and *Empire*." She tapped a finger on the table in rhythm with her words. "If I thought it was necessary, I would sleep fine afterwards. Right now, you are an enemy of the *Republic*."

"And you are a pirate, Keller."

"And you, Dr. Alyona, have never aided pirates before, have you?"

Jessica had matched her scowl for scowl, snarl for snarl, up until this moment. Now, the woman leaned back, blushing furiously as she breathed. Jessica broke the confrontation and leaned back as well.

She felt, rather than saw, Jež relax.

"I am a medical doctor, sworn to help," Dr. Alyona whispered.

"I will hope," Jessica continued, "that this action will not be necessary, because you and I can come to an agreement."

She let the woman work her way through whatever thought processes were necessary to step back from her own brink.

It only took a heartbeat. Jessica was even more impressed with the woman.

"Okay, Keller," she said with a calm, professional air, "that's the stick. What's the carrot?"

Jessica let go a breath she had been unconsciously holding.

"My staff can make a pretty good estimate as to what research of yours was directly related to the events on *2218 Svati Prime*, and not part of your general studies. All of that research on this planet, the data, the materials, the samples, the personal logs, will be transferred to *Auberon* and stored until such time as it is safe to release it to you and the Imperial College of Medicine. It will then be deleted from your records, your backups, everything."

"And where does my oath come into this?" Dr. Alyona said quietly.

The room had gotten very small, very personal. Jessica could only imagine what it would have felt like in a smaller space.

"I want you to supervise the entire operation for me," she said.

She watched the Doctor lean forward angrily, about to lead off with a string of profanities, or possibly something more prosaic, like *Are you out of your mind?*

She subsided into silence instead and leaned back.

Jessica counted the heartbeats.

Dr. Alyona contented herself with sipping her tea, eyes watching Jessica over the rim like a rabbit spotting a hawk.

"Why?" she said finally.

Jessica decided to go with the most honest answer she could. It would help her sleep nights, that way.

"Because my staff is good, Dr. Alyona," she said simply, "but we're not up to your standards as a research university. And you would never forgive me if anything happened to that data. I can't imagine it will be too long before I can return it all to you."

Dr. Alyona got a cagey look in her eyes. "You're up to something," she observed.

Jessica shrugged grandly, mostly for her benefit. "We have been from the very beginning, Dr. Alyona," she said. "You aren't allowed to know what until this all done. Then, I promise I will make it all clear."

For a few moments, Jessica wasn't sure the woman would go for it. This was only partially a bluff on her own part. She could take the time to wipe those records, but if she made any mistakes, she would be answering the Senate rather than the First Lord. And she had many fewer friends there.

Dr. Alyona sighed and put down her tea. She held out her hand for Jessica to take.

"Okay, Command Centurion Keller, my bright-eyed, grown-up pirate," she said, with the faintest taste of something. Warmth? Respect? Hard to tell. "You have my oath."

Jessica felt the knot in her stomach let go. "Thank you, Dr. Alyona. Please, call me Jessica."

"Jessica," she replied, tasting the name. "Call me Yuda."

Jessica smiled and took her hand.

She might just pull this whole thing off, yet.

CHAPTER XXXX

Date of the Republic March 30, 393 Qui-Ping system

The pilot's ready room, down on *Auberon's* Flight Deck, was finally nearly empty.

Jessica waited with Dr. Yuda Alyona, reviewing their final checklists together. Around them, her crew grabbed the last few random crates and hauled them down into the storage chambers deep in *Auberon's* bowels. She'd have compared them to an old wooden sailing ship's bilge, but those ships were plagued by rodents and lacked climate controlled lockers.

Yuda penciled the last item and signed at the bottom. She handed the clipboard over and smiled. "Well, Jessica," she said warmly, "it has certainly been an interesting week. You run a tight ship."

"Thank you, Yuda. I wish we could have done this under less stressful circumstances. I would like to host you sometime for a formal reception, preferably one where I don't have to worry about being stabbed by one of your scientists."

"I'm sure something can be arranged, after all of your secrecy has died down."

Yuda paused to study Jessica's face closely. "Just how long do you expect we'll be detained, Jessica?"

Jessica pointed to a young man who had been trying to stay unobtrusively against one wall. She gestured him to join their conversation. He had a courier's bag at his waist with several key documents in it. Jessica didn't trust this information being carried electronically.

"Yuda, this is Yeoman Naoki Ungaretti," she introduced them formally. "Yeoman. Dr. Alyona of the *Canton* Hospital Ship *St. Albertus Magnus*. Give her all the respect and courtesy you would afford me, while you travel with them."

"Aye, sir," he said politely. He nodded to Yuda. "Doctor, it is a pleasure to meet you. I look forward to voyaging to *Ladaux* with you."

"Yeoman," Alyona replied carefully.

"I don't know the current state of affairs back home, Yuda," Jessica continued. "We've only been to a base once in the last six months, and then just long enough to pick up supplies. I am sending a complete and up-to-date report for the First Lord to read. Nils Kasum will treat you and your staff exceptionally well, and hopefully be able to give you a much better idea than I do. At the very least, you will be detained on the nicest planet in the Republic. More likely, the Republic will hire you to do things in a distant, internal sector while we wait. That was my recommendation."

"I see," Yuda said. "Thank you, Jessica."

Jessica held out a hand, but the bigger woman stepped forward and wrapped her in a hug.

For a moment, Jessica just stood there, uncomfortable and unsure what to do. She took a breath and returned the hug.

When had she last hugged someone?

Jessica stepped back.

Yuda was about to say something when the intercom overrode all speech.

"Squadron, this is Strnad aboard *Auberon*. I have the Flag," Tamara's calm voice boomed out of every speaker in range. "All hands to battle stations."

Jessica took two strides as the voice died down and keyed a microphone on a nearby wall.

"Bridge. Keller. Status?" she said. Behind her, she noticed that Dr. Alyona and Yeoman Ungaretti had drifted along in her wake, pulled by invisible tides.

"Tactical here," Tamara responded instantly. "Imperial Battle Fleet just dropped out of Jumpspace, right at the edge of the gravity well. Closing now."

"How fast, Tamara?" Jessica asked urgently.

"Stand by, sir," came the message, followed by a moment of silence. "Cruising speed, sir. Outer edge of firing range for the Primaries in about eighteen minutes if we sit still, which we aren't. Transponder identifies the Batlteship *IFV Amsel* at the center of the formation."

Cruising speed? Wachturm? He should be coming down her throat as fast as his battleship could move. She would have.

"Roger that, Strnad," Jessica said. "Pick a vector twenty degrees off of his course and start everybody running, emergency flank. Wake Denis up and turn things over to him so you can start planning your defense. I'll be on the Flag bridge in a minute."

Jessica cut the comm and turned to her companions. She held her breath for a second, weighing the options as the situation unfolded. If the Empire had finally found their little hide-out, it was truly time to go home. Just getting out of here alive right now was likely to be touchy.

And she owed Yuda and Admiral Wachturm both for their good opinions of her. Just because everyone was at war, they could still be civilized to one another.

Yes. That was how to handle it.

Jessica smiled at the weight off of her back. It hadn't been much, but it was gone now.

"Yeoman, change of orders," she said decisively. "Hand me your satchel and get to your station. You won't be leaving today."

"Aye, sir," Ungaretti said, shedding the bag and fleeing the room at high speed.

Jessica turned to Yuda with a smile. She opened the satchel and pulled out the folder marked *Project Mischief*. She pulled out the six key pages that detailed what had been done at *2218 Svati Prime*, both times, and handed them to Yuda.

"Since it looks like you are about to be liberated from the terrible, evil pirates by the *Fribourg Empire*, Yuda, I want you to take this with you, and explain everything to the Admiral. Thank him for me as well."

Dr. Alyona studied the pages quickly. Her brow furrowed harder and harder.

She looked up at Jessica confused. "But this is…"

"This is the galaxy's biggest practical joke, Yuda," she said gently. "My evil engineering gnomes cooked it up for me."

"You did nothing?"

"Hit them with a very slightly radioactive snowball. And a raspberry."

"Why are you telling me this now?" the Doctor asked.

"Because we might be killed in a few minutes, and I would like you and the Admiral to know the truth if we are. One less thing on my conscience."

"And you are just giving this to me?"

"You already suspected, Dr. Alyona," she said, "I could see that in your eyes a few times. We didn't act like depraved war criminals or blood-thirsty killers. The game is up. Time to wipe the slate clean and send you home. Good luck."

Jessica took Yuda by the hand and led her through the door as she moved.

Out on the Flight Deck, crewmen were running in every direction as they prepared for the sudden eruption of chaos.

Jessica found the Flight Engineer already at her post. "Iskra, I'm clearing Dr. Alyona and her shuttle for departure. We're leaving them here."

Iskra raised an eyebrow at her as she pushed buttons, but kept her own counsel. She looked at the two women closely and shrugged. "Launch in forty-five seconds, Doctor. Better hurry."

Jessica felt Yuda tug on her hand to face her. The noise around them was growing louder, so she almost had to shout, "Thank you, Jessica," before she turned and raced to the waiting shuttle.

Jessica turned to her Flight Deck Commander. "How soon can we crash-launch everything we have, Iskra?"

"Two minutes after that. Make sure those folks have a working transponder, and let the Imperials know who they are."

Jessica smiled. "They have two captured friendlies and three enemies in close formation. They won't be launching missiles randomly into the mess until they can identify things. Alyona's shuttle will be docked safely by then. I imagine her pilot's going to move like a jackrabbit."

"Agreed. Now what?"

"Now," Jessica said as she turned, "we try to get out of here alive."

CHAPTER XXXXI

"Enej, who's out there and what are they doing?" she called across the space.

Jessica had started talking as soon as the door to the Flag Bridge opened enough for her to squeeze through and race to her chair.

Her Flag Centurion looked like he had just crawled out of bed, wearing sweatpants, fluffy wool socks, and his regular uniform tunic, which had probably been resting over a chair for the morning. This was just about the middle of his usual duty shift night, so she could forgive him. She was up very late herself, just to see Yuda off, so she was about two cups of coffee ahead of him.

"Confirm that we have *IFV Amsel* inbound, sir. That is definitely the Blackbird. Looks like the great white whale finally found us. There's also an Imperial squadron with him. Tentative classification of three frigates and a light cruiser."

"*Amsel* could kill all three of us herself, if she got close enough, Enej," she said simply. "The rest are escorts to keep us from getting uppity."

She slammed into her chair and hooked the various buckles. She didn't always take the time to strap herself in, but there was a good chance they were going to lose power and the gravplates today. Best not to be floating off if that happened.

One finger found the conference function. All of her command staff were present a moment later, floating like light ghosts around the projection of the system.

"Enej," she said, "please add spheres around all ships showing outer effective range of the Primaries, and then a larger sphere for safe Jumpspace."

She took a breath to watch the various balls move around one another. It didn't look promising. But why was he coming in so slow?

"Kigali," she said after a moment, "come in close to *Auberon* and fly a very tight escort for now on a flank. I expect missiles to start soon, timed to get to us about the time Wachturm opens fire with his big guns."

"Roger that, *Auberon*. Executing now." The blond commander had a stern look about him today as he looked aside to talk to his own staff.

"Jež," she continued, "*Auberon's* the slowest. Can we get clear before they can hit us?"

His image shrugged. "If we red-line everything to the point we burn out the engines, sir," he said, "we might be able to get there. I would still expect him to get in a couple of shots when we did, and there won't be anything held back to reinforce the shields."

"Are *St. Albertus Magnus* and *Johannesburg VI* likely to slow him down at all?" Tamara asked.

"Doubtful," d'Maine replied with a gruff growl. "One of his frigates would be enough control both of them. The other escorts will be more than enough for us, unless we sent the entire Wing out and pulled the same kind of maneuver on them as they tried on us at *Ao-Shun* last time. Launch everything we have all at once and try to overwhelm them."

Jessica watched the board unfold. Something didn't feel right, but she couldn't put her finger on it.

Wachturm was better than this.

"Jež," she said, "have Ozolinsh push the engines as hard as he dares, but don't go for broke. We're going to need them later. I'd rather go for evasive maneuvering and hope *Amsel* doesn't hurt us too bad. We don't need to fight, only to escape. He has to come to us."

Enej Zivkovic screwed up his face at her from across the table. "Then why isn't he chasing us harder, commander? They could have been on top of us at emergency flank."

"Because, Flag Centurion," d'Maine replied, "that would have been a knife fight, and we've got a whole bunch more knives than they do. It only takes one lucky shot in a brawl like that. Even against a Battleship. He knows that, over there."

Something about Zivkovic's words spurred Jessica to spin the projection again, until she was looking at her own fleeing squadron from Wachturm's point of view on his own bridge. Something in her brain clicked.

"He's not chasing us, people," she said with a sense of wonder to her voice, "he's driving us."

"Towards what?" d'Maine said. "There's nothing over there."

"Correction," Jež said before she could open her mouth, "there no active transponders or scanner arrays over there. Should we launch *da Vinci* and have her look?"

"Negative, Denis," Jessica said sharply. "If this is a trap, I have a better way to spring it. What's missing from the fleet behind us?"

She noted the confused looks on most of the faces.

Tamara caught on fastest. "A full Task Force like that should have four frigates, a light cruiser, and a heavy cruiser or battlecruiser attached. I can't imagine why he'd leave them behind when hunting us, unless he had them waiting for us someplace like *C'Xindo*."

"He didn't, Tamara. My gut tells me that they're sitting over there, coasting in without engines, sensors, or transponders, right at the edge of safe Jumpspace."

Jessica reached out and touched a spot inside the projection, and then a second, drawing a line from the front of Auberon to the point where their flight path would get them clear of the gravity well.

"Tamara, I would like you to fire a barn owl along this path, ballistically. Just one stealth missile. Set it to arm thirty seconds after it clears us, and have it home in on any signal it receives and run it down. There's nobody friendly in front of us we can hit."

She thought for a second.

"Kigali," she said, "we're just about out of shot missiles, but that fleet doesn't have nearly as many launchers. Still, I'm going to need your team at the top of their game."

She waited for him to nod.

"Jež," she continued, "confirm that every launch rail has a missile on it, and then crash launch the Wing. Put everybody on the same side of us as *CR-264*, just like we were going to try an overload launch, similar to what they did to us at *2218 Svati Prime*. Everyone else, prepare to launch every missile you can get into the air, as fast as possible, when I do call for the fighters to blitz."

Enej actually raised his hand to speak, a concerned look on his face. "I thought the consensus was that they would be expecting us to do that."

"They are, Enej," she said with a hard smile, "expecting it, that is. We shouldn't disappoint them."

She reached down and opened another comm channel. "Engineering. Flag. Please put Moirrey on."

"I'm here, ma'am," the shy voice came back almost instantly.

"Moirrey, I know we left a few surprises for people back at *2218 Svati Prime*," Jessica said. "Do we have anything ready to go right now?"

Moirrey hummed to herself as she thought.

"We've go' one ready a'go now, ma'am," the Yeoman replied, "Could fix a second one in aboouut five minutes."

"Please do, Moirrey. Ozolinsh, if you can hear me, pull anyone she needs except people keeping the engines running."

A faint "Will do," could be heard from across the room.

Jessica closed the comm and looked across at Jež. "We'll use the crash launch to cover it. There will be lots of noise."

"That there will be, sir," he said.

"What about *Rajput*, sir?" d'Maine asked.

"Not a lot for you, d'Maine," she said. "Try to ease a little ahead of us and fade away a bit from our track, like you were getting ready to turn hard and fire a wing shot backwards at them. Be ready to redline and fire everything you have forward, when and if it comes."

"Aye, sir," he smiled harshly. "Right hand holds the big sword."

"Either blade kills, *Rajput*," she replied, "as long as they're sharp."

"We'll be sharp, commander, don't you worry."

She smiled.

Him, she wasn't worried about.

It was the man chasing them.

Jouster let *Bitter Kitten* launch with *da Vinci* in the primary slot today. She had earned it. He was going out the rear bay landing doors with the two big ships and the two surprise packages. He wanted to make sure everything went off with a hitch.

It was strange launching this way, without the huge surge of acceleration behind him. Shuttles and Fleet Lords traveled this way. But Keller had specific instructions she wanted executed.

Jouster didn't think he had anything left to prove to her at this point, but it was good to see things done right, rather than hoping.

Darkness.

Stars.

A single, dim red dwarf in the distance.

Small, gray rock below and behind them, fading as they ran for the edge of the gravity well.

Light the engines softly, bring the nose around and let the craft slide into the middle of the formation, on the right rear wing of an arrowhead. He was the last one to the party. Even *Necromancer* and *Cayenne* were there ahead of him, but they had been needed in position first.

"Flight Wing, this is *Jouster*," he said firmly. "In position and counting down. Estimated thirty seconds to first navigation point."

He checked the scanners again. Nothing ahead of them, even with *da Vinci* scanning, but she couldn't exactly paint a narrow cone to find anything without giving the game away. No, just a series of hard, omni-directional pulses.

Big, bad battleship and consorts closing from the rear. Have to make this look good.

"Flight Wing, we are at first navigation point," he continued, talking to himself in a bored tone. Nice and easy. "I want everybody to space themselves out some, like we were about to snap around and try to jump the Blackbird. A couple of waggles, maybe some flares. Sell it people."

He fit words to deeds and stood his little *Harpoon* on both wingtips in rapid succession, just like someone preparing to go into high-g maneuvering.

"Squadron, this is the Flag," her voice came over the waves. Hard. Tight. But somehow soothing, like she was completely prepared for what was about to happen. That helped. "Stand by."

There was no response. There was no need. Everyone here knew the score. They had been on the other end of that stick recently. *Jouster* focused on his scanner, letting his brain fly the craft in the background.

A flash of light appeared on the screen, right beyond the Jumpspace perimeter. Somebody had just gotten kicked in the face.

"Bingo," *da Vinci* cried over the comm. "All craft, I have a firing lock. Launch now. Repeat. Launch now. *Cry havoc and let slip the dogs of war.*"

Jouster's thumb was already halfway to the firing stud before she spoke. His craft rocked gently as both missiles detached, ignited, and raced downrange.

Ahead of him, he watched the glare as forty-four missiles launched, almost simultaneously.

It was star-bright

What was it Leonidas had said that day? *Fine, then we shall fight in the shade.*

There was a wall of giant, gray arrows falling on the newly-revealed battlecruiser. Truly, enough to shadow the sun. Hopefully, this was going to be more like Crecy than Thermopylae.

Ahead and on the outer wing of the formation, *Rajput* suddenly swiveled in. Two bright lances of energy licked out.

Keller had been right about the Imperials.

But the Republic had come prepared.

Jessica really had hoped she was wrong. That maybe Wachturm was playing it safe and just wanted to chase her away, taking potshots instead of getting into a melee. Possibly, he hadn't heard about the second run at *2218 Svati Prime* yet.

Not even that kind of news traveled very fast across space.

In her heart, she didn't believe it for a moment.

The flash of light on her projection was vindication, of a sort. She had guessed right about the man. He was still a genius.

Now, she had to find out if she was better.

"Giroux," she called to the Science Officer. "Fastest readout, please."

"Roger that, sir," he replied, face down on a screen. "We have an Imperial Battlecruiser playing possum over there, plus a frigate. Cruiser's shields are coming up now, along with his engines. Expect incoming fire shortly. Transponder identifies her as *IFV Muscva*, Capital-class Battlecruiser."

"What about the frigate?" Jež's voice entered the conversation across the open command channel.

"Looks like we scored a direct hit with the stealth missile, sir," he replied. "Caught her with her shields down. She may be off-line. I'm not detecting shields yet."

"Make sure all missiles are tracking the Battlecruiser," Jessica said.

"Aye, sir," somebody replied. It was hard to tell in the noise. Not that it mattered who, as long as it was done.

"Tactical," Jež called, "all available power evenly split fore and aft to the shields, now."

Jessica focused her attention on Wachturm, and the Battleship *Amsel.*

It would take them a few moments to redline the engines even if they had been prepared, but she expected it. She had just called their bluff a little early.

That was still a Battleship.

"Damage Control, stand by," someone called over the general comm. "Incoming fire."

Auberon rocked as if she had just been sideswiped. The very metal of the hull rang like a bell. Even the air turned hazy as dust was vibrated out of cracks.

That was what it felt like when a Primary beam hit you, even with shields.

"Tactical," Jessica said calmly, "who fired that round?"

"That was the cruiser, *Muscva*," Tamara responded. "Battleship is still a little outside of range, unless he gets very lucky."

"Expect him to try, Strnad. There's trouble brewing up here."

"Roger that. Vanek is on her guns."

Jessica watched the projection with trepidation. There wasn't much she could do at this point except count the seconds until the big ship brought her cannon battery to bear. And then, how long they would have to endure it to escape.

If they could.

Muscva fired a second salvo of Primaries while Jessica watched. Three shots missed completely. Two grazed low as *Auberon* had already begun to flare up and away from her previous track.

The last one caught the carrier right in the teeth. She bucked like a wild stallion trying to throw a rider, twisting, rolling, and bucking.

Jessica felt light as the gravplates went down. The entire Flag Bridge went dark, except for the big projector.

She thanked whatever benevolent gods watched over them that they had that much power left.

In slow motion, Jessica watched the Imperial Battlecruiser let loose every Secondary she had at the wall of incoming missiles. Missiles that would have been targeted at the big ships were suddenly fired at incoming missiles, like bullets meeting in mid-flight. The carnage *Muscva* wrought was terrible, but it wasn't nearly enough.

At least a dozen missiles got through and ran home as Jessica watched.

The Imperial Battlecruiser simply disappeared under a wall of flame, explosives detonating and mixing with oxygen and metal from the ship itself.

Jessica frantically pushed comm buttons, but nothing responded.

"Commander," she heard Enej Zivkovic say, groggy or in pain, "I have the Emergency Bridge on the line."

"Em Bridge," she called, "who's on?"

"Centurion Brewster, Commander," he said. Once, her least favorite person, but he had worked hard to redeem himself in her eyes. Now their fate rested on his shoulders.

"Tobias," she said distinctly, "the Bridge and Flag are off-line. You are Tactical Officer until relieved."

"Roger that, sir."

She heard him gulp once. She felt the same.

"What are your orders?"

"The Battlecruiser is dead, Brewster," Jessica said. "Ignore the frigate and get everything ready for missiles and an Imperial Battleship."

"The frigate died with the cruiser, ma'am," she heard him say faintly, "one of those secondary explosions was her going up as well."

"Understood, Brewster," she said, "do not hold anything back. We were four minutes from Jumpspace, when the engines still worked."

"Roger that, Commander," he said quietly before his voice took on a new tone. "I have the Flag."

Jessica looked around the Flag Bridge and tried to orient herself. Damage Control would be furiously fixing things, but were most likely going to be down in Engineering, or up on the Bridge. Nobody would bother with them, just yet.

She detached her restraints and glided across the room, waiting in the back of her mind for the gravplates to come back on and drop her like a stone.

She made it to Zivkovic's station just as someone restored some of the power to the gravplates, dropping her suddenly to her feet. It was barely twenty percent, but it would do.

Jessica pulled her Flag Centurion's head back where she could get a look in the light of the projection. Goose egg on the forehead. Probably slammed his skull into the console when *Auberon* bucked. No blood. Pupils the same size.

"I'm all right," he muttered, trying feebly to pull away from her hands.

"You cracked your head, Enej. Sit tight until we can get you go medbay."

Around her, the hull rattled with a variety of sounds.

War, in all its glory.

Missiles from both tubes as Brewster dueled with a ship several times his firepower. Even the dull thump of one of the Primaries. Had *Amsel* closed already?

Jessica reached under the Flag Centurion's console and found the reset switch. It didn't fix everything, but at least the emergency lights came on, a dull yellowish hue. Jessica sneezed reflexively at all the dust revealed.

With light, she made her way back to her own console and reset it. The Comm to the bridge was still offline, but she could apparently talk to other stations.

She hoped that the silence was caused by a burned out relay, rather than a direct hit that had killed everyone on the bridge.

It was supposed to be protected almost as well as the Flag Bridge, but when your number came up…

She studied the projection in front of her, the only part of the Flag Bridge working at one hundred percent. What she saw astonished her.

CR-264 was still close, trailing in along *Auberon's* side, even as the carrier continued tumbling.

Rajput had somehow shut down her engines, spun on her short axis, and was coasting backwards. Her Primaries lashed out like lightning bolts.

Jessica would have to ask him how he had done that trick. d'Maine was even firing his Type-3s, although hits at this range were rare and soft. Still, anything that kept *Amsel* at bay.

Auberon's own Primary battery fired once. Considering the weapons normally pointed forward, they shouldn't even be able to bear straight back.

She checked the partial readout and realized that *Auberon* was tumbling like a wounded duck through space, engines running fitfully, with apparently at least one of the big gyroscopes off line.

Every time *Auberon* tumbled just right, Brewster was firing a Primary.

Hitting, too, although at this range it was like tickling a bear to death.

Unless they got lucky, *Amsel's* shields could hold out long enough to get a killing salvo in. Unless he wanted them alive.

That thought chilled Jessica even more. Yuda wouldn't have had time to talk to him and tell him about *Project Mischief*.

He might be out for blood.

"Commander, this is Em Bridge," she heard Brewster say. "We're seeing no enemy missiles incoming from the Imperials. Suggestions?"

"Best guess, Brewster," she replied, "they were all set to do to us what we did at *2218 Svati Prime*. Every rack was loaded with shot missiles and they have to be cleared in order to fire ship-killers. We fired everything the wrong way and caught them off guard."

"Roger that, sir. Small blessings. *CR-264* has nothing to do but stay clear of us as we tumble."

In the big, hollow projection, Jessica watched *Jouster* line up the entire Flight Wing in a shape that looked like a cone, tip pointed at the Battleship. Every craft fired at the same moment.

Fascinating. Each individual fighter didn't have nearly enough energy to do much damage against those shields at this range, but collectively, she watched them limn the big ship like St. Elmo's Fire.

They weren't going to kill a Battleship today, but they were going to make him pay a desperately high price for their hides.

With a lurch, the rest of gravplates came back on and lights came full. It was almost blinding after the warm semi-darkness she had been wrapped in.

The comm came live as well.

"Squadron, this is the Flag," she heard Brewster say loudly, "*Auberon* has power again. Time to run."

"Brewster, this is Jež," she heard her First Officer say, "I'll take charge, thank you."

"Negative, Bridge," Jessica overrode their voices. "This is Keller. Brewster has command of *Auberon*. I have been watching things move out there. I have the Flag. Stand by as needed."

She heard a chorus of grumpy assents, but they were all professionals.

And Brewster had managed to score hits on a target at extreme range while tumbling a Strike Carrier. She wasn't sure she knew many others who could have done that. Let alone while under fire.

She checked the projection.

"Engineering, I need emergency flank speed, right now."

"Working on it, sir," Ozolinsh grumbled over the comm. "We are well aware of who the neighbors are."

Auberon shook once like a horse and then steadied.

"Flight Wing, this is *Auberon*," she heard Brewster say over the comm. "Prepare to make an attack run on the Battleship and her escorts."

Jessica caught herself short of overriding him.

If they lost the wing and escaped, it was a terrible-fierce price to pay. But if they lost everything, then the Imperials won, simple as that. Better to salvage what they could.

"*Auberon*, this is *Jouster*," she heard the reply. "It has been an honor to serve with you guys. Good luck."

Jessica ground her teeth as the squadron lined up. Now was time for the *Charge of the Light Brigade* out there.

On the projection, *Amsel* suddenly backlit as if a supernova had erupted behind her.

"Giroux," Brewster called over the comm. "What just happened?"

As she watched, the Imperial Battleship fell off-line and began to wobble awkwardly, like *Auberon* had been moments ago.

"Flight Wing, this is Keller," she said suddenly. "Abort your run. I repeat, Abort your run. Return to base immediately and prepare for Jumpspace."

"Roger that, Flag," *Jouster* called back. "Standing down."

"Flag Bridge, this is Engineering," Moirrey's lilt floated across the air. "Mine number two has magnificently scored a direct hit on the enemy flagship. That design is a success. I will add it to *Project Mischief*."

On the screen, the Battleship's consorts had pulled back to swarm around her defensively, suspecting that someone had manage to sneak up on them.

Auberon was forgotten in the kerfuffle.

Time to run, indeed.

Rajput spun gracefully on her midline as Jessica watched. d'Maine must have turned off the gravplates and cycled several gyroscopes to pull that trick. She had to find out how he did it. That was just an amazingly-rude surprise for someone chasing you.

The gap between fleets began to widen as the Imperials faded. Jessica let out a breath.

"Squadron, this is *Auberon*," she heard Brewster announce proudly, "transition to Jumpspace now. See you at rendezvous *Theta*."

Auberon made the leap. Jessica felt Wachturm's blade miss and slide away behind her.

CHAPTER XXXXII

Date of the Republic March 24, 393 Jumpspace outbound from Qui-Ping system

It was the biggest space where she could comfortably seat enough people.

Jessica filed into the big conference room in Engineering last, as befit her rank, and because the main corridor connecting it to the Flag Bridge was still open to space in places, forcing her to almost circumnavigate the ship to get there. Her command staff was intermingled with a great many engineers, as well as a couple of pilots.

They had saved her the chair at the end. She took it gratefully, doubly so as Marcelle appeared with a fresh mug of coffee.

The room watched her expectantly as she sipped. They could wait. This *was* Marcelle's coffee.

She set the mug down as the warm happiness flowed into her limbs, and eyed the room. Her two evil engineering gnomes were the only two she wanted to talk to, anyway. The rest of the mob was just taking up space.

"Quiet," she growled, stilling the few whispered conversations.

Vanek and Kermode were at the other end of the table, dangerous little pixies. Jessica speared them with a glare, but softened it. Moirrey was smiling bright enough to light up the room, all by herself.

"Normally," Jessica began, loud enough to be heard, "after-action reports are dull, boring affairs, where various officers interview their staff and review logs to go into excruciating detail about what happened, what went wrong, and how to learn from it."

She let the room dangle. The only sound was the air circulating.

"And I'll get around to that, tomorrow. Right now, I would like to ask Moirrey what she did to save our butts from the bogeyman."

All heads rotated like gun turrets. Jessica watched the Yeoman blush furiously and take a deep breath.

"As you know, ma'am," she began, projecting her voice across the room like a stage. Perhaps it was. All the world. "At *Ao-Shun*, we left behind a dozen o' those lovely little orbital mines that look a wee bit like communications satellites. Only these went boom when ya gots too close."

She reached down and fired up a projection of one of those mines.

"I were buildin' a new one that was a bit bigger an' wee smarter," she continued, drifting into a brogue as she worked, "but that one apparently missed, or misfired, or something. No boom. Number two worked."

"Moirrey," Jessica said, "those mines didn't have enough explosives to knock a Battleship that far off line. Maybe a Cruiser if they got lucky. Certainly a Destroyer, but not a Battleship."

"Yus, ma'am," Moirrey replied. "But that tweren't a boom. We fired a Primary round into 'er ass as she went by. Figured she's have all her shields focused for'd an' no be payin' attention. Leave us a soft spot."

Jessica waited for the room to settle down from the nearly-painful eruption of sound. She used a fist on the table top to get everyone to shut up.

"Moirrey," Jessica inquired, "where did you get a Primary shell to use? I don't remember authorizing one to come out of stores."

Jessica fixed her glare on Jež.

His eyes got big and he shook his head forcefully *no*.

"Oh," Moirrey brightened, "Alber' had a discharged round he let us have. Said 'twere bad luck on his ship. Would be good fer ours."

Alber'. Alber'? Command Centurion d'Maine, commander of Rajput? That Alber'?

Jessica fought successfully to keep her face relaxed and her eyebrows out of her hairline.

"I see," she said.

She hadn't, but she was beginning to. The pixie had charm. Dangerous charm. She would need to be watched.

"Okay, people," she yelled before the noise got out of hand. "Official business."

They quieted down, for the most part.

"Everyone in the squadron officially owes Moirrey and Nina a drink for saving our butts. Again."

She watched both women blush as the room cheered.

"Tobias Brewster," she continued, finding him halfway down the table on her left. He looked like he expected a scolding. She smiled instead.

"Brewster, I have good news and bad news for you." She watched his face swell and then collapse. "You did a fantastic job back there, taking charge of the Emergency Bridge, exactly like you were supposed to." He smiled nervously, waiting for the other shoe.

"You also managed to score nine hits in fourteen shots, at extreme range, at maximum deflection aft, from a tumbling Strike Carrier. Tactical Simulator predicts that the average Fleet Gunner would get four. Congratulations on setting a new high score."

She watched his mates slap him on the shoulder and back. He was apparently well liked down there.

"However," she continued.

He cringed.

"I think we're a better ship if you remain down on the Emergency Bridge, but I am promoting you to Emergency Tactical Officer. Functionally Tamara's backup in all things. Good job, Tobias."

The whole room erupted with cheers this time. They went on for several minutes before she rapped her now empty mug for attention.

"And now, people," she yelled, "let me say thank you. We've made the *Fribourg Empire* plenty mad, so we're doing our business. We'll be in drydock for a while when we get home. Remember that you represent the best ship in the Fleet and behave accordingly."

This time, she let the cheers rolls on as she made her way out the door and went to take a nap. It had been one hell of a day.

EPILOGUE

Date of the Republic April 30, 393 Ladaux

Jessica let Marcelle fuss over her best dress uniform and stood still as wrinkles were flattened and imaginary dust wiped off. She smiled when Marcelle turned and did the same to Jež, standing beside her.

His uniform didn't have nearly the awards and citations on it, nor had he had access to a personal steward like Marcelle to handle those things. Maybe she needed to fix that. Or at least suggest it.

Marcelle finally finished her task and fixed them both with hard eyes. "You will not muss them up, you two," she said quietly, fiercely. "If this is an execution, I will not have you looking sloppy on the way."

"Aye, sir," she heard Denis say in all seriousness.

Marcelle stepped back and left them space before the airlock as they waited for it to open on the other side.

"Sir," Denis continued, "have you ever gotten a reception like this from Flight Control?"

"Negative, Denis," she replied. "Normally, we'd be slotted off to a small dock and met by a Quartermaster Yeoman to supervise linking to station power and recycling."

Jessica took a breath. In. Out.

"I have never been docked at a central bay," she continued. "And never been told to wait for the Stationmaster to arrive before they let us out of the lock."

She had also never done something this big before.

"The *Fribourgers* make enough noise that we really are about to be arrested, and walked before the whole fleet in chains as a warning and example?" Denis looked concerned, but not frightened by the prospect.

Jessica considered everything they had done, starting at *2218 Svati Prime* and running up to the raid on *C'Xindo*. Even the near-disaster at *Qui-Ping* had worked out.

What were the chances that she was about to be given a hero's welcome instead?

"That's one scenario," she finally replied quietly. "But I knew that when I ordered the attack on *Ao-Shun*. Court Martial was almost a given." She took a breath. "This feels bigger. We might have actually succeeded in our original mission."

"Well, Command Centurion Keller," he said, "if this is the end, it has been my pleasure to serve with you."

He smiled and stuck out a hand.

She took it fiercely. "There's no way I'm not going down fighting, Denis."

He nodded. "That's what I'm counting on."

A sound interrupted her.

The great bolts holding the hatch were finally retracting. It was a slow, noisy event, designed to make sure everyone in hearing range knew it was happening.

Jessica looked back over her shoulder. Normally, senior officers would be lined up behind her to debark, but today, pride of place had been reserved for Moirrey Kermode. Nina Vanek and Marcelle Travere flanked her, with the entire Flight Wing, in proper uniforms for once, lined up behind that. The rest of her officers were in back.

It looked wrong, but felt so very right.

The big door opened by swinging out into the drydock bay.

Jessica could see Senatorial Gendarme in full uniform lining both sides of the walkway. It did not look pleasant.

Still, she was an officer in the *Republic of Aquitaine Navy*. These people could not intimidate her.

She still knew her duty.

As Jessica stepped across the threshold, she spotted a small cluster of officials where she would normally have expected to find the Supply Yeoman.

First Lord Nils Kasum stood at the center of the group.

The man beside her was one she knew from pictures, but never expected to meet. Why would the Premier of the Republic Senate be standing there?

Beyond them, held back by the Senatorial Gendarme, a large group of people had gathered. They were mostly fleet-types in uniform, but there was also a large ratio of civilians for such a gathering.

Stranger and stranger.

As Jessica stepped into view, the crowd erupted in cheers.

She stood there, in absolute shock, as the First Lord and the Premier stepped forward.

Nils Kasum smiled down at her. The noise was so intense she couldn't hear anything, so she had to read his lips instead.

"Welcome home, Jessica."

ABOUT THE AUTHOR

Blaze Ward writes science fiction in the *Alexandria Station* universe as well as *The Collective*. He also write fantasy stories with several characters and series, from an alternate Rome to epic high fantasy in the desert. You can find out more at his website www.blazeward.com, as well as Facebook, Goodreads, and other places.

Blaze's works are available as ebooks, paper, and audio, and can be found at a variety of online vendors (Kobo, Amazon, and others). His newsletter comes out quarterly, and you can also follow his blog on his website. He really enjoys interacting with fans, and looks forward to any and all questions—even ones about his books!

Never miss a release!
If you'd like to be notified of new releases, sign up for my newsletter.

I only send out newsletters once a quarter, will never spam you, or use your email for nefarious purposes. You can also unsubscribe at any time.
http://www.blazeward.com/newsletter/

Reviews
It's true. Reviews help me sell more books. If you've enjoyed this story, please consider leaving a review of it on your favorite site.

ABOUT KNOTTED ROAD PRESS

Knotted Road Press fiction specializes in dynamic writing set in mysterious, exotic locations.

Knotted Road Press non-fiction publishes autobiographies, business books, cookbooks, and how-to books with unique voices.

Knotted Road Press creates DRM-free ebooks as well as high-quality print books for readers around the world.

With authors in a variety of genres including literary, poetry, mystery, fantasy, and science fiction, Knotted Road Press has something for everyone.

Knotted Road Press
www.KnottedRoadPress.com

Javier sometimes enjoys being a pirate, but he never forgets they made him a slave.

Join him in his adventures with the pirate ship *Storm Gauntlet*.

Part of the *Alexandria Station* universe.

Available at your favorite retailers.

Made in the USA
Charleston, SC
06 August 2015